Suck Suck Suck

Stories

by Brandt Scheidemantel

Goldenhart Press

Pittsburgh

First published in 2025 by Goldenhart Press.

ISBN: 979-8-9993285-0-2

For Cordie

Contents

Te Adora

On her thirteenth birthday, Tea (*tay-uh*) Ganger fractured her forearm. She'd been riding her bicycle down the biggest hill in the neighborhood when a lime green convertible whipped out from behind a sprawling hydrangea. Tea braced reflexively with her left arm, and the bones cracked against the pavement, splintering like toothpicks and poking through her tender skin like tent poles. There were many other injuries—minor sprains, scrapes, bruises—but no concussion (thanks to her helmet).

Six days later, a Sunday in July, Tea awoke from a dream in which an aggressive masked assailant broke every bone in her body with a metal rod, one by one.

That morning, as she dressed for church, Tea didn't choose her usual outfit: stockings, blouse, and dress shoes. She wore tennis shoes, jeans, and a baggy black sweater that completely hid the bright blue plaster cast on her left arm.

Nonetheless, Tea had much to look forward to. She was a beloved leader in her church youth group and enjoyed welcoming new members.

"Tea," said the minister cheerily, "meet Dora."

The three stood in the chapel foyer.

"Dora and her family just moved here from…"

"Nusquam," said Dora, staring at Tea.

"Right," he affirmed. "*Noos-kwam.*"

"Vanitas vanitatum," Dora said, with crisp Latin pronunciation. "Et omnia vanitas."

Tea raised an eyebrow and looked at the minister, who smiled nervously. Dora still hadn't looked away from Tea. She hadn't even blinked.

"Yes, well," mumbled the minister.

Tea smiled encouragingly, but Dora's eyes were cold and vacant, like a fish's.

"Tea will show you around and introduce you to the youth group."

Dora picked a booger, and Tea's stomach turned.

The tour took fifteen minutes. Tea did her best to break the ice, but Dora said nothing. They walked through the chapel, the administrative offices, and the Sunday School rooms. Finally, they crossed the parking lot to the youth center, a modern building with a basketball court and stage.

The service was about to start.

"We're really similar," said Dora.

"What?"

"Like twins."

Dora was two inches shorter than Tea and twenty pounds heavier. She had long blond hair, whereas Tea's was shoulder-length and ruby red. They did, however, both have green eyes.

"Our faith?"

"Our eyes."

"That's true," Tea said reluctantly, "but yours have gold flecks."

Dora got within inches of Tea's face to inspect. She nodded.

Then she pulled up the sleeve of Tea's sweater.

"Please don't touch me."

"What happened?"

"I fell off my bike."

"How painful was it?"

"Why?"

Dora stared for ten long seconds. She sat alone during the service.

Mid-sermon, Tea went to the bathroom. Out the window, she saw Dora in the parking lot. The girl appeared to be slamming her left forearm in a car door. It was a decent distance, so Tea couldn't be sure. But she thought she saw Dora gritting her teeth and screaming in agony. She thought she saw blood and bones.

Tea ran and left the water running. She told no one.

The following Sunday, Tea was feeling more comfortable with her cast, so she wore her dress clothes to church. Though she'd convinced herself that the parking lot scene was a misunderstanding or an illusion, she was still nervous to run into Dora.

Tea settled into her chair as the youth minister began the morning sermon. She was relieved that Dora hadn't showed at the pre-service coffee and doughnuts. She even found herself hoping that the newcomer had disliked the church so much that she would never return.

But when the minister invited a guest to read scripture, Dora appeared from backstage. She wore tennis shoes, jeans, and a baggy black sweater. An exact copy of what Tea had worn the previous week. There was even a sliver of bright blue near her left wrist.

During the second verse, Tea excused herself to the

bathroom. She gripped the porcelain sink with both hands and held back tears. She looked in the mirror. Her eyebrows furrowed with anxiety and confusion.

For a moment, Tea thought she saw gold flecks in her green eyes.

The next Sunday, Tea and Dora wore the same dressy outfit to church, and many commented on the coincidence, particularly the bright blue casts. Most thought it was a cute happenstance. Some said it was a sign they were destined to become great friends. Dora thrived on the attention, and Tea played along with social grace. But inside, she felt anesthetized, as if her soul had been numbed in preparation for invasive, involuntary surgery.

The next Sunday, Tea faked sick. She stayed up all night streaming movies so that she actually did have dark bags under her eyes. She even feigned a convincing hoarse voice and sore throat. Her mom allowed her to stay home.

The next week, Tea got her period and the usual cramps. On Sunday morning, she played up the pain, and though her mother sensed theatrics, she again let her stay home.

When church let out, Tea received a text from her closest friend in youth group.

"I tapped her butt."

"What?"

The friend sent a side profile photo of Dora.

"I thought it was you from behind."

Dora had cut, styled, and colored her hair in a perfect mimic of Tea. Red, straight, and shoulder-length. She was still heavier and shorter, but at a glance, the likeness was striking.

"Photoshop prank?"

"She told me to call her Tea."

"Come on."

"Someone has a crush on you."

"Someone's a crazy loner."

"Did she try to kiss you?"

The rest of the week, Tea was sullen and withdrawn at dinner. Her parents noticed but didn't press at first. She still followed her normal summer schedule. Up early everyday and active with the neighborhood kids. Long hours in the garden and evenings spent reading. All typical except for church.

On Saturday night, Mr. and Mrs. Ganger tested the waters.

"Reverend Paxton is finishing first Samuel tomorrow," said her father.

Tea said nothing.

"You love the story of Saul and David," added her mother.

Silence.

"Tea?" urged her father, sweetly.

"Oh, right. Who doesn't love a jealous, dick-measuring king in fits of murderous rage?"

Her parents held their utensils still.

"Excuse me?" said her father.

"I'm sorry," Tea snapped. "You meant when David rapes Bathsheba, has her father murdered, and takes her mother as his wife, raping her too?"

"Where in the world…"

"Ah, that's second Samuel," Tea chuckled. "My

mistake."

"What in God's name is this?" he said.

"God's dead. He has no name."

"To your room," said her mother.

"I'm not done eating."

"Now."

For the last six weeks of summer, Tea was more isolated than ever before. She did not go to church and spoke only the minimal necessary amount to her mother. To her father, not a word. She had no siblings, and her only pet, a goldfish, had died the previous winter.

Luckily, Tea still had her friend from youth group, who kept in touch via text. After those first few weeks, the friend reported, Dora had stopped attending church. This was a great relief to Tea, who hoped the weirdo had disappeared forever.

Two weeks before school started, Tea and her church friend went shopping. Their moms took them to the mall, and four hours later, the girls had each purchased a considerable back-to-school wardrobe. They were particularly excited about their 'first-day' outfits.

There was a hair salon near the mall exit, and a gorgeous late-twenty-something woman walked out with a fresh bleach-blond bob with bangs. Tea and her friend squealed and jumped up and down. After sufficient begging, Tea's mother asked her own stylist to squeeze the girls in for appointments that week. And despite her misgivings, Mrs. Ganger allowed Tea to get whatever she wanted: an ear-length bob with bangs—dyed black. From ruby red to squid ink. The effect was shocking, but the stylist had done an excellent job. Tea was euphoric.

On the first day, Tea and her friends wore make-up and stylish new clothes that were slightly sexy. Most were teenagers now, and at lunch, they talked about boys. But only Tea had drastically changed her hair, which the girls gushed over. One even wanted a picture, just the two of them, to post online.

"I don't have social media," Tea admitted sheepishly.

All the girls had made accounts over the summer, and they'd been posting and tagging for months. Meanwhile, Tea's father had used a parental control lock to block access.

"Lame," replied a tech-savvy friend.

Within ten minutes, she had undone the lock, created an account for Tea, posted the photo, and tagged her.

"We are so *effing* cute!"

The girls snapped hundreds of photos, and by the end of lunch, Tea was awash in social joy. She and her friends were better dressed than ever and displaying their beauty to the whole online world.

But after lunch, the party stopped.

"Class, I'd like to introduce a new student all the way from…*Nuss-kwam?*"

The class turned slack-jawed to Tea. Then back to Dora at the front of the room. Then to Tea again. Someone laughed. Someone gasped. Others squirmed silently.

Dora had an ear-length bob cut with bangs. Pitch black. She wore the same 'first-day' outfit as Tea, except her shoes were two-inch platforms, putting them at the same height. And Dora had lost twenty pounds, every single extra ounce that had once separated her figure from Tea's. She even had real scars on her left forearm.

Tea tensed into immobility. She wanted to scream. But she also felt as if she might pee her pants or vomit.

Instead, she grabbed her books and ran out of the classroom, knocking Dora's shoulder.

At midnight, Tea received a notification:
'Theodora (Dora) Doppel wants to be your friend!'
Tea clicked on the profile. There were photos of Dora at church dressed like Tea. Photos at the mall. Even at the hair salon. The most recent was with Tea's friend who set up the social media account. She and Dora had snapped a photo after school.

Tea slipped out from under the covers. She walked over to her fish tank and dropped the phone in. It fell right next to the treasure chest, whose bubbly feature had long since broken. After a minute or so, the screen died, and Tea fell sound asleep.

An hour later, treasure chest bubble three times, and the phone turned on. The social media application jumped out of its homepage slot, slid past the other icons, and squeezed itself into the phone's hardware. It was stuck beneath the home button, struggling to find a way out. Finally, the icon broke through and emerged from the phone's charging port.

It stepped into real life. It had little hands and feet.

The icon swam to the surface, scaled the fish tank's glass wall, and shimmied down the wooden dresser. It crept across the pink carpet in the moonlight and climbed Tea's puffy white comforter like a billowy mountain peak. With the stealth of a secret agent, it crossed the canyon of her ear and waded through the black forest of bangs until it peered over the edge of her eyebrows. Then it opened her eyelids and dripped three golden drops into each eye.

Tea awoke and saw her phone in the water. It was

dead, and she was content. She went to the bathroom and started the usual routine. When she checked the mirror, she noticed a glint in her eyes. There were three gold flecks in each green eye. The mirror rippled like a wave, and on its surface, a notification appeared.

'Dorothea (Tea) Ganger has accepted your friend request!"

Tea felt a thumping pressure in her forehead. Her eyes reddened and swelled beyond their sockets. She thought to reach for eye drops, but instead grabbed a metal skincare spatula, which she set against the bridge of her nose. The cold stainless steel tickled her eye.

She prepared to pluck.

"How painful was it?"

Suck Suck Suck

Four days before the octopus sucked him dry, Richard Thompson visited the bank at lunchtime on a sunny Wednesday afternoon. His son George, who was studying abroad in London, had requested money to fund a weekend trip to Barcelona. The fifteen minute errand was hardly an inconvenience. In fact, it allowed time to reflect on the great pleasure of giving his son opportunities that Richard had never had. His own father had squandered the family fortune on extravagant gambling and died in prison. To provide George with financial stability and opportunity was a source of deep personal meaning.

Spain. What might it *smell* like?

The bank's parking lot was full, even the two handicap spaces. But inside there was a teller at every stall, so the line moved quickly. Richard handed over his debit card for account identification, and before he knew it, the transfer had been initiated. On his way out, while putting away the debit card, he noticed his wallet was rather thin.

While I'm here, he thought, it would be prudent to withdraw some pocket cash. Just in case.

In the bank vestibule, Richard inserted his orange plastic debit card into the ATM. He waited a moment for the screen to offer his banking options. When, after ten seconds, the screen hadn't changed, Richard scratched the growing bald spot at the back of his head. He ran a finger over the card entry slot, which was flashing green. Nothing there. Nothing sticking out. He tapped the screen and was prompted to enter an account number for card-free withdrawal, a feature he'd never heard of.

Richard sighed. It seemed the machine had eaten his card. Though he'd heard several such stories, this was his first ride on the merry-go-round. But his frustration was tempered by confidence in the bank and its staff. Richard had been a customer for over thirty years, and the personnel at this particular branch knew him (and his wife and children) by name. He trusted them to recover the card in a timely manner. Perhaps ten or fifteen minutes, tops, which wouldn't interfere with his afternoon work schedule: a solitary review of his direct reports' account reconciliations.

Richard got back in line, occupying his mind with thoughts of his son and Spain.

Would George finally eat octopus? As a boy, Richard had been obsessed with those wild color-changing creatures after watching a marine life documentary. He'd always ordered octopus when the opportunity arose and had been encouraging George to expand his palette for years with no luck.

"Too slimy, Dad. Gross."

This time around, the teller who motioned Richard to her window was Susan Forster, a late-thirties mother of three with a kind, competent demeanor. When she smiled, tiny pleasant creases gathered at the corner of her eyes. They'd known each other going on five years.

"Hi there, Mr. Thompson," she said. "How may I help you today?"

Richard explained about his card, and Susan frowned, as if personally aggrieved by his misfortune.

"I do apologize," she said. "Though we do our best to maintain our machines in full working order, they sometimes malfunction. If you'll have a seat and wait a few minutes, I'll speak with my supervisor, who should be able to retrieve your card."

Richard said that'd be fine and sat in one of the cramped, awkward lobby chairs. There was a plastic coffee machine on the end table. He'd already had a cup that morning, and this month he'd set a goal of decreasing caffeine consumption. But there was a decaf dark roast pod, so he brewed a cup and enjoyed the warm, bitter taste.

Richard had drunk half the styrofoam cup by the time Susan's supervisor appeared. The man wore a light gray suit and a bold red necktie over a white shirt. Everything freshly dry-cleaned. He was in his early thirties and had wavy black hair parted down the middle. There was also a handsome fish-hook scar sliding around his elegant Adam's apple.

"Mr. Thompson," he said, smiling and extending a hand. "I'm Ian Strom, bank supervisor."

Richard stood and shook. Not too firm, not too lax.

"I'm sorry for the trouble with our machine. As I'm sure Susan mentioned, we do our best, but mistakes do happen."

The supervisor smiled uncomfortably, hesitant to deliver bad news.

"Unfortunately, I've searched the ATM in question, but I was unable to locate your card."

"Unable to locate?"

Strom winced, shrinking as if scolded by a motherly tap on the head.

"Yes, I'm afraid so. There were no cards in the

machine."

"I used it not ten minutes ago."

"Yes."

"I placed my card into the flashing green slot, and it disappeared."

"Yes, certainly, right into the appropriate slot."

"But it's not inside?"

"Allow me to be precise, Mr. Thompson. After a thorough search, *I* was unable to locate your card."

Richard balled his hand into a fist and released. He'd never met this spiffy supervisor. In fact, he hadn't spoken to anyone in management since opening George's account a decade back. The bank was so well run that he had never needed to escalate an issue.

Until now.

"What, *precisely*, do you mean?"

"My search, however earnest, was limited by my experience and skill set."

"Your search..." said Richard, choosing his next words carefully. "You're not denying that my card is in the machine?"

Strom frowned pityingly and motioned Richard to sit. They sat, and Richard sipped what remained of his decaf dark roast. Strom gathered his thoughts.

"We do not deny that the debit card in question *may be* located inside this particular machine. Indeed, it is of the utmost importance to our bank that you, Mr. Thompson, our valued customer of thirty-one years, eight months, twelve days, twenty hours," Strom looked at his watch, "six minutes and fifteen seconds, know that we support your belief that the card is in this machine."

Support my belief? Six minutes and fifteen seconds?

Richard finished his coffee with a gulp.

"Unfortunately," Strom continued, "as I'm sure Susan mentioned, malfunctions do occur. Bent cards get stuck. Incompatible foreign cards are inserted, backing up the intake slot. Other more complex mechanisms, wholly unrelated to a customer's card, may break down at any time. Regrettably, while there is only one way for the process to function successfully, there are many ways it can go wrong. That said, as a bank supervisor with nearly ten years experience troubleshooting ATMs across the Western Pennsylvania region, allow me to assure you, Mr. Thompson, that no more thorough a search could have been executed by someone of my skill set than the one which I undertook on your behalf."

Strom beamed, a smile radiating pride. His eyes even sparkled.

Richard brought the empty cup to his lips, concealing a dumbfounded stare.

"Therefore, I would like to propose a further search by our *branch manager*."

Strom's eyebrows danced magically at the words 'branch manager'.

"Actually, I've already taken the liberty of calling her in. Given my inability to fulfill your service request, the gravity of this malfunction, and our commitment to your belief, Mr. Thompson, I felt the situation warranted such attention. She arrives tomorrow morning, so if you'd be so kind as to return in the afternoon, she will have carried out the search by then."

"That can't be necessary," said Richard.

"Mr. Thompson, nothing could be *more* necessary. As a customer of our bank, you deserve the full support of our exceptional customer service. In fact, Mr. Thompson, you've earned it, paid for it. Your loyalty of over three decades is incomparable, especially in this age of limitless consumer choice. You really could bank with anyone else, but you choose to bank with us. It is, therefore, more than our duty. It is our honor to go the extra mile for you, as you have done for us."

"But where could the card possibly have gone?" Richard asked.

Strom nodded.

"As you said, Mr. Thompson, you inserted your card into the machine minutes ago. There is, as you rightly imply, only one place for the card to be. Please do not allow my lack of qualification and skill to cast doubt upon your conviction or diminish your confidence in our bank. Your trust and belief are the most important assets we possess, and we will use all power at our disposal to demonstrate our reciprocal belief in you, Mr. Thompson."

Reciprocal belief? Cast doubt upon my conviction?

The situation had ballooned out of control. Strom was speaking a different language. Richard looked at his watch. Far too much time had passed. He could barely remember why he used the ATM in the first place. Best to head home, put this odd encounter out of mind, and finish the day's work.

"Can't I just have a new debit card made?"

"Certainly, Mr. Thompson."

"Let's do that."

"As you wish. I'll have the new card shipped to the home address on file. It should arrive in two to three business days."

"Thank you," said Richard, tossing the styrofoam cup and standing.

"All the same, Mr. Thompson," said Strom, shaking hands with intent, "I encourage you to return tomorrow afternoon and speak with the branch manager. Your account is *very* important to us."

For the rest of the afternoon, Richard worked from his home office, reviewing his team's account reconciliations for the recently completed fiscal year. Usually, he worked at the company office, leaving his door open. As managing director, it was important to be visible and available to his direct reports. But this firm was smaller and local, so he enjoyed a certain flexibility compared to his early career in big corporate accounting. Working from home one afternoon was no problem, especially if it minimized distractions and improved focus. Before long, he settled into a steady rhythm and managed to accomplish his daily goal, despite the delay at the bank.

Richard's wife and daughter were on a long weekend trip in the mountains. George was in Europe. So other than the black tabby cat, Céline, Richard was alone. For dinner, he wrapped a Yukon gold potato in foil and thawed a sirloin steak. He grilled both over an open flame and washed them down with an ice-cold beer. It was fall, and the leaves were changing in their brilliant ways. Richard reminded himself to set aside time this weekend to service the leaf-blower. The previous year, he and the kids had spent two full days raking, but it hadn't built as much camaraderie as he'd hoped. It had simply been a chore.

Richard opened a second beer, surprising himself. He hadn't done this since his early twenties. He cracked the cap off a frosty bottle and swallowed a refreshing mouthful. He wanted to let his mind wander peacefully, to think about his son in Barcelona, about salty, paper-thin *jamón serrano* and plump, paprika'd *pulpo a la plancha*.

Would the leaves be changing there too?

But all Richard could think about was his missing debit card and the malfunctioning machine. He hadn't even *needed* the pocket cash. If push came to shove, he kept some bills stashed around the house, and it wasn't as if he planned to buy drugs. Richard had six credit cards, all viable options to purchase anything these days. Still, he had surrendered his card to the machine. And, according to Ian Strom, experienced bank supervisor, it had mysteriously disappeared.

None of that bothered Richard, though. Rather, it was the supervisor's strange words that stuck in his mind like a sharp fish hook. *Reciprocal belief.* What could that possibly mean? And who was this bank manager? What sort of skills might she possess that Strom lacked? And really, just what was inside that ATM anyway?

As Richard slid into bed, he still hadn't decided whether he would go to the bank the following afternoon. The more he mulled over the decision, the muddier his mind got. He counted sheep under the covers for nearly an hour before finally dozing off.

That night, Richard dreamt he was a fish hook. Down down down he descended, deep into the Mediterranean sea. For the longest time, it was empty and peaceful down there. No light. No sound. Only the shadowy pulse of sea creatures swimming in their mysterious ways. The line was weighted at the top, but down there, Richard the Hook hovered, weightless and free, a bright pink lure enveloped in a harmless darkness. Then an octopus beak clamped around him, and he awoke in a cold sweat.

Decades ago, Richard used to dream vividly. He had one recurring childhood dream in particular: in the center of a spring meadow bloomed a massive willow tree, whose delicate branches enveloped a huddle of infant fauna. In safety and comfort, the animals sipped from a mountain-fed stream that abutted the willow's thick trunk. A swift wind rustled budding leaves as Richard gathered food nearby. With provisions in hand, he crossed the stream, and the cold fresh water rushed over his bare feet, waking him.

But that was then.

It had been years since he'd dreamt anything at all.

Certainly nothing new, not since puberty.

The next morning, Richard chose not to think of the fish hook dream. He showered off the cold sweat and dressed for work. As usual, he read the local paper at breakfast. One piece of ever-so-slightly-burnt whole-wheat toast and a sunny-side-up egg. He punctured the plump yolk and lapped up the dribbly, golden goop. He brewed decaf, a rare choice. It was typically only after lunch that he switched off the caffeine. This little challenge helped him avoid thoughts of the dream, the ATM, and his tentative afternoon meeting at the bank.

At the office, Richard's morning was filled with meetings. First, the weekly all-staff for general announcements and an introduction to the new head of HR. Then, three back-to-back quarterly performance reviews with his direct reports. These one-on-one meetings lasted a half-hour, and Richard dedicated about a quarter hour to review each meeting itself: what productive, critical feedback did I provide? Were the next quarter's goals clear, challenging, and set and agreed upon by the direct report themself? And finally, did I offer an open forum for concerns and did I listen—truly *listen* —to my employees?

The morning ended before it began, and Richard was extremely tired. And hungry, too. It had taken him many years to learn how valuable these meetings could be and to accept the necessary sacrifice of time and energy. Most employees, he'd found, got frustrated when they didn't have clear goals or when they didn't understand how their personal goals related to team goals. Patiently explaining the complicated, opaque tangle of organizational goals dispelled confusion. Listening to frustrations and collaborating on solutions improved his team's happiness, which boosted productivity. It was simple in concept but time-consuming and extremely draining in practice, which was why so many managers never bothered. Most performed perfunctory, ineffective yearly reviews that placated their own higher-ups. These managers still achieved success, leading by example, working longer and harder, no matter how unclear their vision or inefficient their efforts. But they also churned through employees like a propeller through plankton.

Not Richard, and he took pride in that.

As usual, on days without a lunch meeting, Richard ate alone. Today, he was glad of it. His hunger was biting, and he couldn't wait to order a foot-long roast beef hoagie on white. Extra mayo, too. It was mid-afternoon by the time he slipped away to Tony's Hoagies. The bank was next door, and he still hadn't decided whether to meet the manager. This indecision was unsettling, so much so that he considered choosing a different lunch spot, one far from the bank.

Nonsense, he told himself. *I've nothing to fear. I'll stick to my routine and enjoy a hoagie. I can decide about the meeting after lunch.*

But in the Tony's Hoagies parking lot, it was decided for him. In a most peculiar way.

Richard saw the vehicle once he exited his own. In one of the bank's handicap parking spots sat an extraordinarily shiny, bubble-gum pink Lamborghini convertible. It had twenty-eight-inch chrome rims with tires thin enough to hula-hoop, a sharp gaudy tail-fin, white leather seats, and kitsch eyelash extension decals on the headlights. Richard could even see a pair of pink fluffy dice whose numbered dots must have been an opalescent material. They hung from the rear-view mirror, glinting in the sunlight, twirling like some ominous cubes of fate.

That was the bank manager's car. He knew it.

In his many years as an accountant, Richard had never relied on instinct or intuition. In life, he'd used it just twice. Once, to choose his wife. The second time, to pick the numbers on a lottery ticket he'd purchased on his fiftieth birthday. They had just *felt right*. Still, he lost. Otherwise, Richard relied on logic, pure systematic logic. Deductive reasoning squashed divine inspiration. In fact, the latter probably didn't exist. Not in Richard's world. But the sight of this extraterrestrial automobile catapulted a novel sensation to his gut. It was at once a terrific feeling of logical certainty and passionate irrationality. Rather than fight with one another, these forces achieved a unity that inspired and revealed.

Richard was compelled to seek the bank manager.

Tony's Hoagies served high-quality sandwiches. Freshly-baked bread and organic meats and toppings. Locally-sourced produce and homemade sauces. It was a stand-out in the world of chain hoagie joints that dished processed slop worthy of FDA investigation. But for all its virtues, Tony's was chronically understaffed, and that afternoon was no different. Only one teenager managed the whole operation. He ran the register, prepared the sandwiches, took phone calls for pick-up orders and was supposed to clean tables, too. Naturally, the place was a mess, like a packed cafeteria suddenly deserted, plates and cups and half-eaten sandwiches on every table, trash scattered on the floor.

The teen was a thin, tattooed, slightly nervous type, but overall a good kid. Richard always engaged in small talk and left a reasonable tip.

That day, he brought up the car.

"Wild, right?" the kid answered, excited. "The lady paid for a six-inch hoagie with a hundred-dollar bill. Then she left another hundred in the tip jar."

He wiggled the plastic jar, showing off his prize.

"The driver was a woman?"

"She was dressed up like the car, so I figured…"

"You spoke with her?"

"You know me," he said. "I'll talk to anybody. She said she's the bank manager."

"But you've never seen her before?"

"Nope."

"You're sure?"

"Who could forget a car like that? Or those legs?" he said with a sly grin.

Richard sat at a window table overlooking the bank parking lot. His hoagie had plenty of mayonnaise but tasted dry and flavorless. He sipped his diet soda sparingly, eyes scanning like a swimmer in shark-infested waters. Why did he suddenly feel so vulnerable?

However long it took, whatever happened, he would meet this bank manager. Account reconciliations could be completed at night or even over the weekend. His wife and daughter wouldn't be home for four more days. George was on his way to one of the world's great cities. And Richard, the fifty-six-year-old accountant with a secret stash of Rogaine in his vanity cabinet, was about to meet the bank manager.

He ate the whole footlong without taking his eyes off the shiny, fluffy dice.

After lunch, Richard parked in the middle row of the bank's parking lot, right behind the handicap spot containing the Lamborghini. Foot traffic in and out of the bank passed the pink monstrosity. To Richard's surprise, no one stopped to stare. No one even took a second look. Somehow they swallowed this image as an ordinary part of their lives.

Richard read the license plate: $UGAR MAMA. He took a deep breath and unbuckled his seatbelt. His throat felt suddenly very dry, and he reached for the radio's volume knob. Anything to distract himself from the nausea pulsing through his body. But he decided against it. What if some horrific catastrophe had occurred and the gory, depressing details were being broadcast on all stations? That would only make this situation worse. He took one last deep breath and entered the bank.

Susan Forster, the pleasant teller, recognized Richard as he walked in. She waved and smiled from her post at the drive-thru window. She wore a headset and was placing documents in a pressurized tube. Before Richard could wave back, he was approached by the bank supervisor, Ian Strom.

"Mr. Thompson," Strom smiled. "We're grateful you've decided to return this afternoon."

Richard hadn't even stepped off the entryway rug. It was as if Strom had been waiting for him, ready to pull him into the bank like a powerful undersea current.

"I'm thrilled to report that progress has been made on your case. If you'll follow me, I can escort you to the office of our bank manager where she will provide further details."

Strom wore a navy suit, a charcoal gray tie, and a new white shirt, freshly starched. His black hair had the same part, and Richard noted the fish hook scar, whose pinkish color seemed to have darkened a shade overnight. Strom led him past the lobby furniture to a small office.

The room was bare, as if it were a cheap showroom of what a furnished office might look like. One L-shaped desk, a high-backed swivel chair, and two low chairs on the opposite side. Shelves with fake potted plants along one wall, an unframed canvas print of a sunrise on another, and on the third, two windows with a view to the parking lot. With a crane of the neck, Richard could see one of the Lamborghini's long-lashed headlights.

There were three personal objects on the desk, all bubble-gum pink: a ceramic mug with a tea tag over the side, a picture frame with feathery pink fluff around the edges (turned away from Richard), and a laptop in a hard enamel case.

"Please have a seat, Mr. Thompson," said Strom. "I'll inform the manager of your arrival."

"Thank you."

Halfway out the door, Strom bit his lip. Then turned. "Also, please know that my manager has spent hours this morning with our machine, laboring to retrieve your card. The progress she has made is truly innovative, an inspiration. I say this not only as a humble pupil who has learned a great deal from observation, but also as an advocate for you, Mr. Thompson, and your belief. If you'll be patient while I alert her to your presence, I'm certain you'll be most satisfied with her findings."

Richard nodded, and Strom beamed, this time bowing slightly from the hips before leaving.

Progress? Hours?

Either the debit card was in the machine or it wasn't. To Richard, this didn't seem like the type of situation where progress applied. Certainly not one that required hours to address. Then again, perhaps ATMs were more complex than he knew. Richard had assembled and disassembled enough lawn-care appliances and household gadgets to know how easily a simple, quick fix could turn into a day-long project. This ATM might very well be the same. Who knows what missing parts, hidden wiring, or quirky design flaws might be lurking inside.

While waiting, Richard felt an urgent, painful desire to look at the picture frame. What image might it hold? Of her? If she had one, of her family? Perhaps a beloved pet? Maybe a shot of the Lamborghini as she first drove it off the lot? A bank manager who owned a vehicle such as this...what motivated her each day? It was a terrible temptation to resist, but he held out. He didn't want to get caught snooping.

Richard's eyes were shut with concentrated self-denial when she finally entered. He first noticed her perfume, a mysterious combination of sweet vanilla, brackish seaweed, and smoky ink. She walked briskly, passing his seat before Richard could brace the armchair to stand.

"Mr. Thompson," she waved a hand. "Stay seated."

She appeared to be in her early forties and wore her

blond hair in a neat, tight bun. Her make-up was simple, clean, and professional. Not too much. Not too little. She had small, graceful wrinkles at the corners of her eyes and had not had any work done. Her excellent posture filled out a well-fitted pink pantsuit of a shiny, high-quality fabric, one that Richard's wife would have been able to identify. She held a designer pen (also pink) in one hand and nothing in the other. She wore no rings. The only jewelry she did wear happened to be the one element that struck Richard as out of balance with such a refined, professional look: colossal silver hoop earrings.

The manager placed her pen adjacent to the laptop, straightened the picture frame, and adjusted the angle of her laptop screen. Only after organizing her workspace did she finally make eye contact with Richard. Her eyes were an arresting blue, like a deep dark hole in the ocean.

"I assume, as a professional courtesy, that you have many pressing responsibilities. As such, I will aim to be more direct than my counterpart, Mr. Strom. However, if this curt disposition discomforts you, you need only say so."

She paused. Richard was still a bit lost in her eyes, so she waited.

"That's fine," he said with a dazed tone. Only once he spoke did Richard realize the full effect of her stunning beauty.

"My name is Sharon Charon. I manage this branch, among others in the Western Pennsylvania and Ohio region."

She paused again.

"That's Sharon, as in *share-in*. Charon, as in *sure-on*. Not *share-in share-in*, as many a low-life tormenter has cat called. It's extremely important that you understand this detail, Mr. Thompson. Sharon Charon. I am not a slut, especially not because I wear big hoop earrings. Is that clear?"

Richard nodded. Or had he shaken his head?

Slut? What was she talking about?

"I'll take that silent, confused nod as an indication that you've never worked with a woman like me before. So be it. To demonstrate your compliance, please say my name."

Richard correctly said her name.

"Very well. Now that we've established the parameters of our working relationship, let's cut to the chase."

Sharon Charon slid a small orange piece of plastic across the desk. It was half of a debit card with the name Ricardo on it. In the space between the first and last name, the card had been sliced in two, as if by a precise laser. Richard picked the card up and ran his thumb over the partial black magnetic strip.

"Thanks to the diligent work of Mr. Strom and several hours of concentrated effort on my part, I was able to locate and retrieve half of your debit card from our machine."

Richard turned the card over again and again. He kept saying the name Ricardo in his head.

"This isn't my card."

Sharon Charon arched an eyebrow.

"Not your card?"

"My name is Richard. Not Ricardo."

Sharon Charon narrowed her eyes suspiciously. She turned to the laptop and ran her fingers across the keys.

"Ricardo Thompson," she said, following with his account details: current address, phone number, date of birth, occupation, Social Security number.

Richard's stomach turned.

"Most recent transaction…a withdrawal," she named the amount, "transferred to your son's account, also a customer of this bank."

Sharon Charon turned the laptop toward Richard.

"Withdrawals and deposits of similar amounts over the past three years," she stated. "I'm assuming based on your son's age in our system that you are supporting him through college, Mr. Thompson?"

"My name is Richard Thompson," he said. "*Richard.*"

Sharon Charon exhaled, pinching the bridge of her nose.

"Mr. Thompson, I am a busy woman, and while I am by contract dedicated to providing exceptional service, my resources are limited, particularly my time and patience. The supervisor of this branch, Mr. Strom, one of my most promising direct reports, called me in especially to handle your case. Only at considerable expense to our institution and through the sweat of my finely threaded eyebrows have I been able to recover half of your debit card from our machine. This half," she held up the orange plastic, "matches the existing account number and personal information linked to your checking account. Do you deny the transactions between you and your son?"

"No." How could he deny them? Richard had felt fatherly pride with each deposit.

"What you are then implying, Mr. Thompson - and rest assured I take this implication bordering on accusation *very* seriously - is that there is a critical flaw in our machine, one at a deeper level than that to which my initial search penetrated."

Richard was too confused to speak.

"You're implying that our machine not only snatched your card and failed to dispense your funds, but that it also somehow altered your legal name in the process?"

"Yes," he said hurriedly. "That must be the case."

Though how could he be sure of anything anymore? The transfers were irrefutable.

Sharon Charon wheeled back and laid her palms flat on the desk. Richard felt her gaze pierce his flesh. The air in the room grew stuffy, and the lights dimmed. Slowly, deliberately, she removed one hoop earring. Then the other. She undid her bun, allowing the long blond strands to fall over her shoulders.

"Well, Mr. Thompson," said Sharon Charon, sucking her teeth. "Looks like I'll be sticking around this branch longer than I anticipated."

She placed the earrings in a bottom drawer and removed a slender ergonomic pillow, which she inserted between the small of her back and the swivel chair. She stretched her neck, exhaled, and slid the laptop square between the pointy padded shoulders of her pretty pink pantsuit.

"We'll be happy to have you back tomorrow afternoon, Mr. Thompson," she said with a sarcastic edge, "by which time I will have an update on your case."

Richard wanted to say something, to yell maybe, or plead for an audience. He wanted to tell Sharon Charon that she had been far too direct, even mean. He needed more of her time, some compassion, and a bit of respect, too. But she had already begun furiously typing.

"As ever," said Sharon Charon, eyes on the screen, "our bank is dedicated to your belief and will stop at nothing to provide you with the most excellent service as is within our power."

"I…"

"Have a nice day."

That night, Richard grilled again. Atlantic salmon and asparagus with fresh squeezed lemon and shaved parmesan cheese. He sat on the back deck and chewed slowly. The leaves were one step further on their journey, speckled with brown spots like a whale shark. His wife had sent a photo of their daughter roasting marshmallows around a campfire. No news from George in Barcelona, but that was to be expected. He was twenty-one, single, well-funded, and abroad.

Richard drank whisky before bed. Two two-finger glasses of a peaty scotch. Neat with a splash of water. He didn't want to sleep. He feared that he'd dream about the fish hook again. And he did, only this time the darkness was deeper, the passing shadows larger. The beak not only clamped down but broke the thick line. Richard the Hook fell out of the octopuses's mouth, down down down to where no light had ever been, down beyond the silent peace, down beyond the pitch-black emptiness, down into those hostile pressurized depths where black sulfuric mineral clouds of terrified rage bubbled out of chemical chimneys in the vented alien ocean floor.

Richard woke with a start again. This time he felt he'd been falling from an awful height, and it took his legs a minute to catch up to his body, which lay harmlessly flat in bed. He couldn't recall what he'd been dreaming about, but he figured it must have been a serious nightmare. He immediately reached for his phone and called in sick. His secretary was shocked. In the seven years she'd worked for Richard, he'd never once called off. "Your voice sounds very weak," she said, truly worried. "Rest up this weekend, Mr. Thompson." He assured her he would and asked that his meetings be rescheduled for the following Friday. In case of emergencies or minor approvals, he would be available intermittently via email.

Intermittently.

Never in his career had Richard operated under such vague, uncertain conditions. He shrunk under the covers, putting a hand to his forehead. This was exactly the lack of clarity that he'd seen ruin so many teams. Maybe. Perhaps. Sometime. Intermittently. But what other choice did he have under such conditions? He felt the lingering confusion from yesterday's mysterious meeting with Sharon Charon and a dread of their next encounter. Yet he knew he had to go.

The morning fell apart. Richard burnt two pieces of toast so badly, he couldn't scrape them back to life. He dropped his sunny-side egg on the floor, splattering yolk on the hardwood cabinetry. Céline licked up the mess and miaowed, but Richard was too preoccupied to realize she needed fed. Eventually, he served himself a bowl of sugary cereal, his daughter's preferred breakfast. He also brewed an entire pot of full-bodied, caffeinated coffee. He even used heavy cream and sugar. The morning paper lay forgotten on the front stoop.

Seated in the breakfast nook, Richard drank cup after cup of coffee and watched fallen leaves tumble across the lawn. They seemed so at ease to be blown around, dead, decaying, tossed here and there by the wind, wherever it happened to want them. Some flew up and over the fence, out of his yard. Others got trapped in the gutter or under a bush. Beneath the brilliant, sunny, cloudless sky, everything seemed so clear. So harmless and simple.

But Richard couldn't sit there, staring uselessly until the afternoon.

Without showering, shaving, or even brushing his teeth, Richard threw on sweats, a tattered t-shirt, and tennis shoes. He went to the garage. In the empty space where his wife's car normally sat, he unfurled a bright blue tarp and carefully flattened its wavy surface. Once satisfied, he dragged a rickety 50cc motorbike out of the shed. It was a beginner model bequeathed by his wife's uncle, deceased now eleven years. Richard had kept it, intending to fulfill young George's desire for speed and adventure. But when the bike didn't start, it spent a winter in the shed, and his son's enthusiasm for motocross turned out to be a passing childhood curiosity. The bike had been gathering dust ever since. Still, Richard had always meant to get it to start.

Today, of course, was the day for this most important task.

By noon, half the bike had been disassembled, and the parts were arranged meticulously on the tarp. Richard had changed the spark plug, replaced the fuel line, and cleaned the air filter. Still, the engine wouldn't turn over. He fiddled with the ignition and considered rewiring some of the electronics. This little two-stroke engine, effectively a lawn mower, wasn't so complicated, but the electronics were well outside his area of expertise. Any imprecise meddling could be costly, so he paused for lunch.

Richard was sweaty, oily, and hungry. He made a sandwich with lunch meat, spread three handfuls of potato chips into a bowl, and pulled two sweet n' sour pickles from a jar. He ate standing at the kitchen island.

Best not to sit down and start wondering, he thought.

Just then, Céline, the black tabby, rubbed her high-arched back against his leg and miaowed. Richard interpreted this as affectionate agreement with his thoughts, but really the cat was dreadfully hungry.

When he returned to the garage, Richard inspected his work. He'd made progress, improving the bike's overall readiness to ride, but the engine was still dead. He'd anticipated that. Perhaps the problem was located inside the combustion chamber, whose crankshaft and piston were as foreign to him as life in the deepest ocean, that faraway place where in dreams he flirted with predatory cephalopods of celestial proportions.

Richard needed to kill time without killing the bike. Anything to avoid thoughts of Sharon Charon. He decided to number and categorize the parts where they lay on the tarp. He placed a piece of tan masking tape next to each and labeled it with a thick, fuming sharpie. On some level, Richard knew this was silly. Eventually, he'd call his brother-in-law, a mechanic with twenty years experience, who would fix the bike in an hour. Who knows, maybe even five minutes? Ever since inheriting the clunker, Richard had meant to do so. But this unnecessary taxonomy, created patiently and logically, calmed his nerves and successfully occupied his mind.

For a time.

The sun descended across the tarp.

Oh no, Richard thought, looking at the clock.

Sharon Charon is *expecting* me.

Like a river unleashed to the sea, its ancient dam undone by a sudden earthquake, Richard's heart burst forth, drowning fearful evasiveness with an all-consuming, blind, roaring hope. He ran into the house and cleaned himself up, thinking now only of Sharon Charon.

Richard arrived just before closing time, and the bank was packed. He had to park at Tony's and walk over. There was the $UGAR MAMA, secure in its handicap spot. He ran a finger over each pointy eyelash of the headlights and whistled.

The line of toe-tapping customers was nearly out the door. It seemed many people had waited until the last minute to make a pre-weekend trip to the bank. Susan was too busy to greet him, and Strom, occupied with another customer, simply motioned toward the manager's office.

The afternoon sun shone across the lobby and landed in front of Sharon Charon's office, where Richard paused to collect himself.

"I smell you," said Sharon Charon. Her voice was cold with disgust.

Richard presented himself sheepishly, and Sharon Charon looked him up and down with disappointment. She pointed to a chair, and Richard sat, perplexed by a deep feeling of shame.

"Mr. Tomazón," she said. "Are you aware that you are *drenched* in aftershave?"

"Toma-wha?"

"We'll get to your name later, Mr. Tomazón," said Sharon Charon. "Right now, I need you to focus. You are drenched in aftershave. Do you know that? This is a bank, not a nightclub. Why have you shined your shoes? Why in God's name are you wearing cufflinks and a gold watch? And, is that, *gel* in your thinning hair? In twenty-four hours, you've completely altered your appearance, and although this bank's primary concern is with your belief, let me remind you of the parameters of our working relationship, Mr. Tomazón. I am Sharon Charon, and I am not a slut."

Sharon Charon's pen struck the desk like a deep sea oil pylon drilling the ocean floor.

"Am I getting *through* to you?"

Richard couldn't think straight. He smelled himself. She was right. God, it was an obnoxious stench. He looked at his gold watch and cuff links and shiny shoes and the reflection of his shellacked hair in the window. Christ, he was wearing the suit he'd worn to the symphony with his wife on their anniversary. How had this happened? Had he been in such a rush that he didn't notice what clothes he'd chosen?

"Forget it," said Sharon Charon. "However suspicious or foolish I might personally find your behavior, Mr. Tomazón, it does nothing to affect your trustworthiness in the eyes of this institution. Onto the matter of your card. You will be pleased to learn that your debit card was in our machine after all."

Sharon Charon slid an orange plastic debit card across the desk. It was whole and had been issued to a Ricardo Tomazón. Richard read the name several times, then looked helplessly into Sharon Charon's bottomless blue eyes.

"Why the long face, *Ricardo*?" she said. "I'd have thought you'd be relieved. Your belief is confirmed. Vindicated, Mr. Tomazón! Our ATM ate your card. You were right to press Mr. Strom on his failed search, and you were right to persist at the sight of your incomplete card. The flaw had indeed been located in our system at a depth which I knew only in theory. Through the long dark night—over seventeen hours, Mr. Tomazón, *seventeen*—I slaved, groping through unknown layers of our machine, applying my limited knowledge, failing, learning, failing again, until I brought the issue to light."

Sharon Charon held up her left hand, as if introducing evidence.

"I even broke a nail," she said.

The ring finger nail had been halved vertically, nearly to the nailbed, where a remaining sliver curled like a barbed fish hook against the inflamed flesh.

"An extremely painful process. Painful, Mr. Tomazón. I have *suffered* to secure your belief."

Sharon Charon exhaled and slowly lay her hand flat on the desk. With the other, she brushed a stray hair back from her forehead.

"Of course," she said, indignant scowl melting into professional smile, "we are honored to provide you, Mr. Tomazón, our customer of more than three decades, with the most excellent service available in our industry today, and we hope you will think of us for all your future banking needs."

Richard had been staring at Sharon Charon's breasts for some time. They were, quite like the rest of her bodily features, sensational. Since she'd addressed him as *Ricardo,* he hadn't heard a word. In fact, he hadn't listened or paid much attention since entering the room. He'd failed to notice Sharon Charon's shiny new black pantsuit and its bubble-gum pink pocket square, patterned with little black octopuses. Instead, he was laser-focused on the tiniest amount of visible cleavage.

"Mr. Tomazón," said Sharon Charon, noting his gaze. "I had no expectations for this assignment. A job for me is a job. Efficiency, precision, accountability, integrity, service. If anything, I was curious about your particular situation, given that Mr. Strom could not handle the request. He truly is my most promising direct report, the most self-directed employee I've ever managed. One performance review, just one in thirteen years with our bank, that's all he's ever requested, and candidly - manager to manager, Mr. Tomazón - he didn't require even that. Time will make a fine bank manager of him, and more. That said, I want you to know I consider you a despicable coward and lecherous trickster. Although our system contained a flaw, you and your card carry a significant portion of the culpability for this malfunction. I don't know how you managed to fool Mr. Strom, Mrs. Forster, or any other member of our staff into calling you Richard Thompson, but it ends here, Mr. Tomazón. It ends now."

Sharon Charon jammed her pen to the desk once more, shaking the ocean floor.

"But Miss Charon," he said.

"It's *mizz*," said Sharon Charon, sharp and merciless as a harpoon piercing whale blubber.

"Ms. Charon," he corrected. "I'm Richard Thompson."

"Enough."

"Why would I lie about my name?"

"Are you insinuating that your perverse imagination should be my responsibility?"

"What? No, I..." he said. "I mean, what could I possibly have to gain?"

"Mr. Tomazón, I don't care to know what warped pleasure you derive from deceiving my staff. But you will no longer take advantage of the fine institution to which I've dedicated my career. The game is over. The jig is up. The cat is dead and bleeding in the bag. No one knows how it got in, Mr. Tomazón, and they never really cared to see it come out in the first place. If you wish to remain a customer of this bank, you will take responsibility for the account under your legal name."

Sharon Charon turned the laptop screen. There he was. Picture, account number, current balance, transaction history, contact information. All under Ricardo Tomazón.

Richard took out his wallet, fumbling for his license and credit cards.

"Look," he said, tossing them one by one on the desk.

"Stop it, Mr. Tomazón."

"Look!"

Sharon Charon read his license and shook her head.

"Pathetic."

Richard turned it around and felt a miserable, blood-curdling vertigo.

It read Ricardo Tomazón.

"You make me sick," she said.

"No," he begged. "No please, wait. Please."

Richard frantically flipped through his other cards, but they had all been issued to Ricardo Tomazón. The room started spinning. He saw the $UGAR MAMA through the window, the fuzzy picture frame, the sunrise painting, the fake plants, and Sharon Charon in her exquisite, professional beauty. All color swirled and coalesced in his vision, as if tossed into a blender with bubble-gum pink milk. What had been light turned shadow, and the cheap, low-backed chair beneath him felt as though it hovered off the ground. He closed his eyes, desperately holding his breath. His brain felt tight, like its protective skull might suddenly implode.

"Let's eat hoagies!" he blurted out. His voice had

made a two-octave, pubescent leap.

Sharon Charon's face contorted, fearful and revolted.

"Mr. Tomazón, are you *well*?"

"No," he said. "Soy Ricardo. Me llamo Ricardo, por favor. Te quiero. Te necesito. Ámame. Bésame. ¡Gózame ya!"

"Mr. Tomazón, I do not speak Spanish," said Sharon Charon. "And frankly, I have my doubts about your ability to do so. You've proven yourself a cunning deceiver, and I have no interest in who you may or may not *really* be, behind your name."

Sharon Charon broke eye contact and turned to her laptop.

"Ms. Charon, please, I..."

"There's no need to feign such concern, Mr. Tomazón. The card has been retrieved. The identity of its owner confirmed. The machine in question debugged. Consider the issue resolved. In the eyes of this bank, so long as you act in accordance with your legal name, Ricardo Tomazón, it will be our enduring honor to serve you, our valued customer."

"Ms. Charon, I need you."

"As bank manager, I am at your disposal."

"No," he said. "I need *you*."

Sharon Charon stiffened. She straightened her pantsuit and took a deep breath, turning glacially slow to face him. Their eyes met, and her tough expression slackened.

Had Richard noticed a blush?

"Ricardo Tomazón, are you requesting to alter the parameters of our working relationship?"

"Sí."

Sharon Charon chuckled, but she quickly controlled

herself. Richard's heart leapt. He'd made her laugh! Oh to survive the night and live a day under the bright hot sun!

"This is extremely unprofessional," Sharon Charon murmured, wiping imaginary dust off her lap. "A threat to my career progression. Unorthodox."

"Give me a chance."

"You've overstepped."

"Please."

"This isn't the place or time."

"I have to have you."

Sharon Charon scrutinized Richard all over, taking her time to inspect every nook and cranny of his face: the droopy forehead, the stray hairs jutting out of his nostrils and ears, pores the size of craters, the shellacked comb-over, the tight collar bunching his chubby neck, a silly dimpled chin and short bulbous nose, the weight of the years in half-moon shadows under his eyes and finally into those firm, chestnut irises. Sharon Charon peered into them, searching their foundation, sifting for confirmation of the deceit which she'd witnessed on the job. Was it there?

"Return at noon on Sunday," she said.

"Must I wait so long?" he asked, reaching out to her.

Sharon Charon wheeled back in her chair.

"Mr. Tomazón, the bank closes in five minutes."

Richard never sped while driving. Nor had he ever increased the stereo volume past halfway. But leaving the bank at dusk, he was triumphant. He screeched the tires as he swung his beloved silver late-nineties retractable-roof Saab out of the bank parking lot. Roof down, open to the heavens, he blasted whatever his favorite indie radio station happened to be playing: *Never, Never Gonna Give*

You Up by CAKE, a cover of Barry White.

Friday traffic was at a standstill, backed up like tankers in the Suez Canal. Some drivers honked aggressively. Others threw up their hands in helpless frustration. An accident between an eighteen-wheeler full of feminine sanitary products and a pick-up truck packed with aquarium sand had commuters backed up for miles. In this sea of long, troubled faces floated Richard, grinning and lipsyncing to his travel companions.

Richard got home, parked, left the garage door open, and ran upstairs. He threw his best, most expensive clothes on the bedroom floor in a crumpled pile. No matter. He would buy better ones tomorrow. In his underwear, he went to the basement gym. George had regularly used the dumbbells to stay in shape during soccer season. Never Richard. But now he curled his biceps and pressed his chest, baring his teeth, willing dormant testosterone to the surface. He strained and strained until his weak wobbly shoulder joints were numb with pain. He went back upstairs and flexed before the bathroom mirror. Too small, he thought. He ran to his office computer and ordered anabolic steroids but even with express delivery they wouldn't arrive until Monday. Fifty push ups before bed, he thought. And fifty when I wake, and another fifty per hour until Sunday at noon.

For dinner, Richard grilled two sirloin steaks. No veggies. He washed them down with an extra dry gin martini, a little dirty with three Spanish olives. This had been the preferred drink of his grandfather, who had killed many Japanese in the Pacific before settling into a peaceful, prosperous life as an accountant. Richard didn't believe in what he couldn't see. But as a boy he had once looked into his grandfather's eyes and there, behind the muddy brown irises, he'd sensed a strength that terrified his childish innocence. Could his grandfather see him now? Could anyone? Was he Richard Thompson or Ricardo Tomazón?

Richard drank three more martinis, all doubles. He didn't want to be aware. He fell asleep on the living room sofa, splayed out in his white oversized underwear. Céline miaowed and miaowed. The poor domesticated feline hadn't eaten since Thursday night.

Richard woke in the night, severely dehydrated. At least he hadn't dreamt. He drank three glasses of water and read the clock: 3:15AM. A pale full moon shone blueish light across the kitchen. He took two ibuprofen and ran upstairs. He dressed in a wrinkly gray sweatsuit and well-worn slip-on loafers. He didn't bother to change his underwear. In a white plastic grocery bag, he packed two bananas, two apples, a piece of hard cheddar cheese, a granola bar, and two sleeves of saltine crackers. From the fridge in the garage, he grabbed a one-gallon jug of water and a carton of high-pulp orange juice. He left his phone and wallet on the bedstand.

It was nearly 3:50 AM when Richard parked at Tony's Hoagies, overlooking the bank. The parking lot was deserted. As were the lots of all the businesses along this retail thruway. On the road, he'd passed one lonely sedan with its golden fog lights on. Otherwise, the suburb slept in darkness, dotted here and there with commercial signage, like phosphorescent sea critters in an abyssal trench.

Richard had been full of nerves, wondering whether the $UGAR MAMA might still be parked at the bank. But no, it had disappeared. He settled into the driver's seat, removed the seat belt, and reclined by twenty degrees. He peeled a banana and ate half. He gulped down some orange juice and chased with a swig of water. He had no plan other than to wait, which might have frustrated him were it not for the buddy cop TV shows of his youth. He had a romantic vision of stakeouts, a waiting game where two companions shot the shit and with patience, eventually got their man. In this case, Richard was after a woman and had no buddy. The only companion he could conjure was a two-CD set of Glenn Gould playing Bach's *The Well-Tempered Clavier Books I & II.*

During his studies at a small liberal arts college, Richard had been forced to take one non-business, arts-focused subject. He chose a freshman survey course on the history of classical music, mostly because the other choices—language, dance, painting, photography, etc—were frighteningly foreign. At least he knew he enjoyed music. Mostly rock or pop, but that was okay. Nothing wrong with The Beatles and Led Zeppelin, a bit of The Moody Blues, maybe. That semester, the professor touched on many influential composers, from the Renaissance through the mid-twentieth century. For Richard, the only one that clicked was Bach. The composer's fugues and preludes produced a sense of order and harmony, akin to what Richard felt when balancing debits and credits, as if ideas, musical or otherwise, had clear beginnings and ends.

At 4:00 AM on a slapdash stake-out, that music was the only way Richard could stomach his otherwise inexplicable behavior. He stared at the bank, almost unblinking, waiting for the $UGAR MAMA to appear. What would he do if it did? Would he approach Sharon Charon? What would he say? What if she wasn't alone? What if the Lamborghini never appeared at all? Stuffed in the driver's seat, his aging body ached, and his eyes reddened with fatigue. But he did not lose focus.

The sun rose, and traffic picked up.

The CD set lasted three and a half hours. Richard passed the time, tracking the fugue subjects as they danced playfully, following one another like lovers in call and response, whispering sweet nothings. Gould, the pianist on the recording, played with extraordinary precision and delicacy, or so a layman like Richard felt. He hadn't listened to a single other recording. He'd been satisfied with this CD for thirty-some years. Why was that?

When Strom pulled up to open the bank, Richard put on a baseball cap and slid the lid down over his forehead. He checked himself in the fold-down mirror. The stubble he'd grown had gathered stray bits of banana and granola. Wrappers, apple cores, and banana peels were spread across the passenger seat, tossed on the floor, not even placed in the plastic grocery bag. There was a two-liter bottle half-filled with rusty yellow pee. Saltine crumbs spilled into every crevice like beach sand. Bach ran from the top. Ragged with obsession, Richard waited.

But by 11:30 AM, the $UGAR MAMA hadn't appeared. All the customers had left, and only Strom's car remained. Richard was distraught. His patience hadn't paid off. He couldn't wait another twenty-four hours. He needed a glimpse of Sharon Charon. He needed answers.

Strom exited the bank, and Richard gathered himself, straightening his hair, rubbing his teeth with one finger, pulling up his sweatpants, removing the cap.

Suddenly, there was a knock on the window, and Richard jumped.

"You can't sleep here, man."

It was the skinny, tattooed kid from Tony's Hoagies. Richard rolled down the window.

"Woah, sorry Mr. Thompson," he said, "didn't recognize you, sir."

"What did you call me?" he grumbled, bloodshot eyes trembling.

"Sir?"

Richard rolled up the window and looked back at the bank.

The lot was empty.

Richard spent the afternoon downtown, outfitting himself in the finest formal wear and cologne. He purchased a top-shelf gin for himself. But what might Sharon Charon drink? He took one of everything, even the exotic mixers and liqueurs, just in case. He bought three flower arrangements, each hand-picked and filled with lush fragrant blossoms. He would choose which of the three to give when the time *felt* right. His trunk was filled to the brim. He paid a small fortune for a haircut and shave, done by a secretive old Italian man with tobacco-stained fingers whose ultra-sharp straight razor left his face porcelain-smooth. He even got a men's facial at an exclusive spa for wealthy socialite women, several of whom made a pass at him.

Richard was brimming with confidence, certain that this was the best version of himself he'd ever produced, that he ever *could* produce.

For dinner, one steak and one martini. No need to overdo it, he thought. He was fully outfitted and had done an intensive round of dumbbell exercises. He tried to think of what he would say, writing opening remarks and flowery compliments on lined paper. But anything he composed fell flat, and he crumpled the sheets. It was finally time to rely on intuition, to be creative. After that, all he could do was hope that Sharon Charon would accept his proposal to alter the parameters of their working relationship.

That night, his wife called twice and left voicemails. His daughter texted. George even emailed a picture of himself eating *pulpo a la plancha* at a stall in *La Boquería*, Barcelona's famous market. His son had finally tried octopus! But Richard ignored all of them, even Céline, who hadn't been fed since Friday morning's stray egg yolk. The poor captive was painfully vocal, but the more she miaowed, the less Richard seemed to notice.

Before bed, he stood in front of the bathroom mirror.

"Yo soy Ricardo Tomazón," he said.

He took a deep breath, pushed his shoulders back, puffed up his chest.

"Tomazón. Ricardo. Ricardo. Tomazón."

Richard slept a peaceful, dreamless eight hours. He cooked breakfast with precision and calm. He enjoyed a cup of caffeine-free herbal tea and savored the crispy toast and nutritious yolk. The sun shone brightly across the breakfast nook, and there wasn't a single cloud in the sky. He watched the leaves with admiration. Many branches were bare, foreshadowing the winter to come. All was in order.

Just before noon, Richard pulled up to the bank and breathed a sigh of relief. There it was in the handicap spot, the $UGAR MAMA. He left the Saab carrying a handle of gin and the pinkest flower arrangement, one with long-stemmed birds-of-paradise and dark-green palm fronds. Nestled in the center was a slender black velvet box containing a set of genuine pearls straight from the deep blue sea. He swaggered to the front door, which had been left open.

In the vestibule, Richard looked at the ATM that had eaten his card and felt a wave of fondness. The home screen was the same as always, welcoming, beckoning. The card slot flashed green. He set the gin and flowers down and ran his fingers across the metallic number pad. The screen seemed to shine one tick brighter at his touch. The cash slot whirred, purring as if sorting thousands and thousands of bills. The mystery of how this machine had changed his name would remain forever in darkness, but he was content to make his home in that uncertainty, even grateful.

Richard placed the retrieved debit card in the ATM. It seemed like the right thing to do. Out of respect, perhaps. The vestibule grew warm, and on screen appeared a yellow smiley face sporting a bullfighter's *montera* and a Dalí mustache. It winked and from speakers in the ceiling spoke in Strom's pleasant voice: *Bienvenido Señor Tomazón.*

Richard couldn't have expected such a response. But he wasn't surprised either. There were forces at work in this world, even in his quiet little suburb, even at this formerly ordinary bank, far beyond his ability to understand. And though it had altered his identity, Richard did not believe that the ATM meant him any harm. If anything, it felt like an old friend, one that would always remember who he was.

"Hola amigo," replied Ricardo Tomazón, cementing his fate.

He was right about the ATM. It meant no harm. It was much more concerned with the mood. It lowered sun shades on all the bank's windows, even the atrium ceiling. The lobby doors swung open, and a low fog of dry ice crawled into the vestibule. Over the lobby furniture a massive spinning disco ball descended. White strobe lights whirled, flashing on the teller stations, then the offices, then the coffee machine, then the safety deposit boxes and the vault door. Somewhere a subwoofer came alive, and out of the bank's sound system sang the voice of Sharon Charon:

Why don't you do right?

It was seductive, smooth, and pregnant with desire, antithetical to the cold, professional tone Ricardo had previously experienced. The singing was accompanied by a bouncing beat, Gramophonedzie's electro swing cover of 1930s jazz hit *Why Don't You Do Right?* The music was so loud it pulsed right through his body and synced with his accelerating heartbeat. He felt his eyelids flutter and got a rock hard erection, which he made no effort to conceal.

Ricardo loosened his hips and swayed through the lobby. He shimmied his shoulders and bounced on the balls of his feet. In all his years, he'd never been to a disco. Look at him now. He set the flowers on the lobby table as an offering and gazed up into the sparkling disco ball. He lost himself to dance, twirling like a dervish.

Sharon Charon's office door spread itself slowly, emitting a bubble-gum aura, which drew Ricardo's gaze. He adjusted his tie, ran a hand over his impeccably cut balding head, and gripped the handle of gin. He danced on over with a confident grin. But the room was empty. No Sharon Charon. He slowed the sway of his hips.

Ricardo searched the room. The ceramic mug had been replaced by a crystal cocktail glass filled with a pink concoction. Rows of pink fuzzy dice covered the shelves where the potted plants once sat. The two low chairs were gone. In their place was a pink leather futon over which Sharon Charon's black pantsuit, blouse, stockings, and bright tiny white lace panties had been draped. Ricardo fell to his knees and touched each article of clothing. He rubbed the panties between his fingers and brought them to his nose and sniffed.

Ricardo turned to the canvas print, which was no longer a sunrise. It was now a pointillist oil-on-canvas of Sharon Charon posing on the hood of the $UGAR MAMA. She made a kissy face and held pink dice in front of her otherwise bare breasts. Round her neck hung a string of pearls, identical to Ricardo's gift but black as squid ink. He leaned in close, as if through proximity he might decipher some hidden meaning. No luck. Only paint fumes. It hadn't yet dried.

The laptop was open. It showed the account of Ricardo Tomazón: $0. A transfer in the exact amount of his existing balance had been executed only minutes before into the account of Sharon Charon, bank manager. Ricardo laughed, a hysterical unhinged hiccuping laughter. He drank gin from the bottle, spilling fiery pine down his gullet. He ought to have read the transfer details more carefully. He ought to have looked at the second name on Sharon Charon's joint account. It was his wife's. But Ricardo Tomazón had already jumped to his conclusion.

"Games," he whispered. "She likes games the minx, the seductress, the *slut.*"

And the moment the word left his mouth, an octopus leapt out of the fuzzy-framed picture on Sharon Charon's desk. The living breathing enormous sea creature wrapped its powerful pinkish-red appendages around

Ricardo's close-shaved face. It spilled viscous venomous paralyzing saliva everywhere and sucked with all its might, careful not to pierce flesh with its sharp beak. It needed him alive. It wanted something buried down his throat, something deep in his lungs, down down down there. Down beyond words that had never been spoken, down beyond all speech that ever could be spoken.

Down down down.

The beast overwhelmed Ricardo's weak, neglected accountant's body and throttled him to the floor, sucking to the electro beat, sucking mouth-to-mouth, sucking with its eight suction-cupped arms, sucking through his clothes, through his pores. Deep into every nook and cranny of his pitiful vascular system.

Suck. Suck. Suck.

Down off the shelf fell the fluffy pink dice.

Suck. Suck. Suck.

Ricardo didn't panic. He didn't even struggle. Finally, he knew the contents of the picture frame. Finally, he had seen the ocean deep with his own eyes. That burning desire would haunt him no more. It was his octopus, after all. If only my boy could see me now, he thought. I never did reply to his email. I wonder if he did it just to make me happy. Or did Jorge really enjoy eating *pulpo a la plancha*?

Suck. Suck. Suck.

A Plumbing Problem

On the evening of his twelfth birthday, altar boy Álvaro Bandono was raped. Father Fickoft, the man whom Álvaro believed closest to God, bent his pupil over the moonlit altar in the heart of the cathedral sanctuary. The stench of sweat mingled with incense, and pleasurable moans, groans, and grunts echoed in the gothic arches like a foul fugue, drowning out Álvaro's terrified weeping. The prayerful goodwill of the congregation, accumulated during evening mass just hours before, dissipated into nothingness. Saints in stained-glass bore witness, as did the wooden image of long-suffering Christ.

The priest deposited his seed.

Done was the fleshy deed.

Álvaro broke in two. One part, spirit. One part, body. The spirit immediately fled the sanctuary, zipped across the church, dove into an electrical outlet, and disappeared deep into the church's plumbing...more on that later.

First, the body.

Álvaro's spiritless body lived out his orphaned young adulthood getting passed around charities like a lifeless fleshlight, equally pitied and punished for his emotional outbursts and repeatedly taken advantage of by men in authority. Sometimes religious, sometimes not. Eventually, he turned to drugs to numb the pain, and once a legal adult, he drifted from town to town, job to job. He tried to stick to women, even married a woman he admired and adored. But time and again, he slept with men, never certain if this was his nature or a perversion born of the priest's misdeed.

Despite his earnest striving to live a straight life, Álvaro cheated one too many times on his wife, and they separated. Guilt overwhelmed him. He fled to yet another town and fell into even more addictive, more destructive drugs. He started turning tricks to fund the habit and contracted diseases. He lost weight. He lost teeth. His skin took on a translucent pallor. Finally, one of his wealthier clients developed feelings and paid for an extended stay at a ritzy treatment center.

It didn't work.

Though Álvaro sobered up, fixed his diet, and regained some muscle, his psychological problems persisted. He loathed himself and humanity, equally. God, he felt, had betrayed him at every turn, and society had no need of another wounded, addicted, confused, unskilled, resentful, *possibly* gay man.

He was, he told himself, irredeemably dirty.

So he hoarded a handful of ritzy rehab pills and ended his life.

At Álvaro's nearly unattended funeral in the parish church, Father Fickoft did not miss the opportunity to publicly express grief while condemning the former altar boy's wayward lifestyle. He urged compassion and respect for the homosexuals in the church who fail to live in Christ. No matter how hard a shepherd works, Fickoft lamented, tears in his eyes, some of the flock will wander. We must soldier on. We must continue to believe.

As it happened, Fickoft was bugging the current altar

boy, too.

Soldiering on alright.

Now, back to the spirit part.

On the night of the rape, after Álvaro's spirit split from its body, it began a journey through the Other Side. First, the massless jumble of energy sought refuge in a new home. Any nearby object in the cathedral would do: the candlesticks, the linens, the organ, even the wooden Christ.

But everything had been blessed by Father Fickoft.

Like a rogue pinball, Álvaro's spirit bounced off accursed surfaces to no avail, until he slipped into the prong of an electrical outlet. His spirit zipped through the church's electrical lines and into the main circuit breaker, where it got lost in the wiring. After several trips up and down dead-end wires, it found one that led, via a control panel, into the hot water tank.

Álvaro took the form of bubbles shaped like his old face.

But he wasn't alone.

"Jesus's Cheez-Its!" exclaimed another group of bubbles.

Álvaro, terrified and fragile as he was, hid in a corner of the tank.

"Hey, hey! Relax. I've just never seen a sorrier-looking spirit. I mean *damn*, who pissed in your pity pouch, Pocahontas?"

Álvaro had only recently been violated. He was indeed down on himself, so he wept.

"Father Fic…he…he…"

"Ah, faithful old Fickoft gave you a taste of Moses's fleshy staff, eh? Snake bit you in the Garden? Spear pierced the innocent flesh? Eh? Priestly pipe probed your plumbing? Eh? *Eh?*"

This voice chuckled, and Álvaro snarled.

"You…whatever you are, you're twisted."

"The name's Ricky, kid. Richard Lachvoll Freistimme, to be proper. But call me Ricky. Look, don't take this whole rape thing personally. Trust me you're not the first, and I doubt you'll be the last."

"So he did the same to you."

"No! Woah! *Nooooo*, mama. I've been here for decades, way before Father Frisky Fingers. Years and years. Not that Time matters here."

"So where are the others?"

"Others?"

"If I'm not the first…"

"Oh right. Sure, they're gone. Moved on. Passed over. Consummated their function. Insert euphemism here. *Poof!* Disappeared into Death."

"Then why are you still here?"

Ricky made six-shooters of his fists and fired two imaginary shots.

"*Pew! Pew!* Christ on a cross, you fire heaters for such a depressed mug. But hey, yes, you're spot on: I'm still here. I'm what's called an unrepentant spirit. Unlike your cohort of innocent victims whose energy is based on, say, the sorrow of abandonment or vengeful rage, I run on recalcitrance."

"Recalcitrance?"

"Re-*cal*-citrance! I ain't never gonna bend no knee no how! Never! Cause I ain't done nothin' wrong. Not really. Sally Jenkins wanted to fool around *just* as bad as I did. And if Father Fiddle Phallus can bend *you* over the altar, what's a quick christening in the confessional? A blow job in the Lord's Tunnel of Love? I ask you! Man alive! I ask! Besides, *she* was a year older than *me*. If I laid on the smooth talk a bit thick, it's not like she was helpless. I say! Man! All fun and games until Sally moans like Pavarotti choking on a golf ball. Well, then the confessional door swings open and her legs swing closed and its 'Oh, Ricky tricked me! Forced me! Help! Help!!'"

"Did you…?"

"Force her? Wouldn't that be *convenient!* I did no such thing. I took the fall, sure. And she saved face. Probably became a damn nun."

"Then you should be able to leave, move on, whatever."

"In theory," Ricky frowned. "Problem is, I *know* it was wrong to get sexy in the booth. I know that part at least. I shouldn't have been there in the first place. Plenty of other places to do the deed. Plenty of other locales to plow old Sal."

Álvaro grimaced. "Do you have to talk like that?"

"Christ's hot cross buns, you're some kind of priss."

Álvaro narrowed his eyes in anger.

"Right, right. I'm being insensitive. You're fresh off the altar."

Álvaro widened his eyes in rage.

"Sorry! Really, sorry. I'm *just* saying. I'm here because I can neither let go of the injustice nor ask for forgiveness. I'm cursed. Cursed!"

"No, you're not. You're proud."

Ricky grinned and fired another imaginary shot from his hip.

"*Pow!* Bullseye. But hey, at least I'm funny."

Álvaro shook his head with disapproval.

"Come on, *eh?* Somebody's gotta be the laugh factory

in this hot water Hell hole. Huh? Am I right? Huh? *Huh?*"

Ricky leaned toward his new pal, and Álvaro recoiled.

"What's the matter, kid? Cat got your tongue? Frog got your balls? Priest got your penis?"

That last remark broke Álvaro, who flew into a rage and chased Ricky around, screaming.

"Hey! Hey! Calm *down*. Do you really want to spend eternity at each other's throats?"

Álvaro felt sick at the thought of spending another minute with this spirit.

"That's what I thought," said Ricky.

"I've got to get out of here," mumbled Álvaro.

"Bingo!"

"Enough. Don't speak."

"Rawr, *rawr*. Kitty got claws."

Álvaro scowled.

"Don't be cross, boss. Let your pal Ricky help. I've got experience, after all. Think of how many spirits have already come my way before passing over."

"I'll find my own way, *thank you*," said Álvaro.

Ricky whistled. "Suit yourself sassy."

Twenty human years later—either an eternity or a minute to these spirits—Álvaro hadn't made any progress on an exit strategy. Begrudgingly, he swallowed his pride and swam across the hot water tank.

"Hey."

Ricky pretended to have his eyes closed.

"Ricky."

Ricky shifted slightly, as if a buzzing fly were disturbing his peaceful rest.

"I *know* spirits don't sleep. I've been here long enough..."

Ricky grinned and popped an eye open. "Oh? Yet you haven't managed to leave?"

Álvaro sneered.

"Because I can't figure out how."

"Is that so?"

"You already know that."

"I don't *know* anything, if you don't tell me."

Álvaro rolled his eyes. "Come on. Tell me how to pass over."

Ricky impersonated Jack Nicholson from *A Few Good Men*: "you have to ask me *nicely*."

Álvaro gritted his teeth. *"Please."*

Ricky smirked.

"Fine. First, determine where you are and accept it. You're stuck in a pit of traumatic memory—and you're not even in the flesh anymore. Can you *believe* it? How does the trauma get encoded and carried if there's no *flesh*? I mean really! Wow! Next, after you've located yourself and achieved acceptance, it's time to let go of that shattered faith, the rage, the wallowing self-pity. It wasn't personal! God rapes *thousands, tens of thousands* of His children through His servants. Probably more. It's *really* not personal. Neither is the shuffling of priests from parish to parish. All part of the plan. Like the Holocaust or the Great Leap Forward or American slavery or that Soviet famine or Unit 731 or the…"

"That's not God."

"Let's stay focused on getting you out of here. Keep it practical, okay?"

"I will not let you talk about God that way."

Ricky sighed. "Suit yourself. Did God make the Devil?"

"You aren't worth this debate. Just don't blaspheme

my God."

"Your God. My God. God's God. Yahweh, *nah*-weh. At a certain point, a word is a word is a sign is a symbol…yada yada yada…we're all in the cave and none of this is real…nothingness and Buddha and I'm a Zen poet addicted to haikus about ginko leaves. Anywho…"

"Are you done? I'm waiting," said Álvaro.

"What's your drag name, diva?"

Álvaro snarled.

Ricky laughed. "You've got two ways out of here. Number One: laugh. Number Two: haunt. What'll it be?"

"Laugh?"

"That's the immediate path. Straight shot to peace. Onward to Requiem. Eternal rest. The Great Gig in the Sky. The Cloudy Clubhouse. Or Satan's Six-Inch Salami Salon, who knows."

"Come on."

"Just wanted to see if you're paying attention. Ready?"

"For Heaven's sake, Ricky."

"Not for their sake, kid. For *yours*."

"Tell me the way out!"

"Okay, okay. There is a principle, which, if you manage to adopt it, will immediately liberate you."

"I just *adopt* a principle?"

"That's not as simple as you might think."

"Well, what is it?"

"God finds your suffering hilarious. That's what you have to wrap your head around."

"You want me to believe that not only was my rape 'not personal' but it was also, in the eyes of God, *hilarious?*"

"It's tricky. I'll admit," said Ricky.

Álvaro sat in disgusted silence.

"Hear me out."

"God *laughed* while I was being raped?"

"*And* He cried, kid. Think back to when you had a body, didn't you ever notice the similarities, physiologically speaking, between extreme laughter and extreme sobbing? It's all the same to God. Two sides, one coin. Butterfly wings fluttering, first in light, then in shadow. The yin, the yang. The chin, the chang. Even, dare I say, the ding and the dong."

Álvaro shook his head. "You're a useless fool. What do *you* know of physiology? You don't even have a body!"

"I used to! Besides, you think *your* body is so different from God's?"

"God doesn't have a body!"

"Seen Him lately have you?"

"Who *gives* you these ideas?"

Ricky grinned. "Who do you think?"

"Demons. Witches."

Ricky howled with laughter. "Lucifer himself, eh?"

"Probably!"

"Without whom there'd be no humanity, no freewill, nothing."

"So we're back here."

"Always seems to come to that."

"No wonder you've been abandoned to this hunk of old tin."

"That hurt," said Ricky, genuinely somber.

Álvaro rolled his eyes.

"Believe what you want, kid. But I *do* feel the pain of loneliness. Especially here."

"Where's my violin?" said Álvaro, feigning pity,

bowing a tiny imaginary instrument.

"If you're not able or willing to laugh, there's Option Two."

"Haunt?"

"Yes. You must haunt the priest."

"Give me a break."

"Become a vengeful spirit and tip the scales of justice."

"That's absurd."

"Absurd would be if Father Fickoft had called you Mr. President while stuffing his..."

"You're a perverted monster."

"Perversion. Derangement. Madness. Bedfellows of absurdity, holy fountain of comedy."

"You say this with pride."

"I don't say it *with* anything. I state it with all the neutrality of a rising or setting sun. It just is. Besides, isn't it the priest who's deranged? Maybe whatever inspired him?"

"Inspired? It was an act of Evil."

"So, the Devil."

"I'm not doing this again."

"And who inspired the Devil?"

"Ricky."

"Come on, play along."

"My inability to comprehend the necessity of Evil is the foundation of my humility. Yours, I see, is the source of a corrosive arrogance. That you simultaneously play the joker doesn't make you some kind of hero."

"A penetrating analysis. Penetrating! So deeply penetrating its bursting my thirsty pipes...oh...oh...oh daddy...*ohhhhh!*"

"Unbearable. I can't stay here."

"You've said that."

"Isn't there an Option Three?"

"You could mope until Christ comes to change your pity-soaked diaper."

"You think you're really funny, don't you?"

"If I'm funny, I owe a great debt to your majesty for such rich material."

"My pain isn't funny. Not to me. Rape isn't funny, especially when perpetrated by a priest. Option One is not going to happen. Ever. But I will *not* stay here stuck in self-pity. If only to spite you, I will pursue Option Two."

"Here, here. Good man. I say. Hi Ho!"

"How do I haunt the priest?"

"Prepare yourself for a shocking idea: Will it."

"Will it?"

"Yes, focus your desire on haunting the aggressor and the path will manifest itself."

"Just like that?"

"You have to go deep within. Focus and focus some more. Concentrate on your desire for spiritual resolution until your whole heart is pressurized into a diamond of pure Will."

"Then what happens?"

"How should I know?"

"What? You said you've seen spirits pass this way before."

"I have. I watched them wail and rage, and the majority were so obsessed with vengance that they harnessed enough energy to escape."

"But you don't know what happens after that."

"I've never been through the process myself."

"Otherwise, you wouldn't be here."

"Bingo."

"So how do you know I'll pass over after the haunting? How do I complete the process?"

"You'll just have to find out for yourself, won't you?"

"You're not very helpful, are you?"

"Aw, shucks. You really *do* like me."

"I don't even *know* you."

"Hey, that's true. You never told me your name."

Álvaro sneered. "Blessed am I, even in dark places."

"You're one snarky puppy."

"And you are a buffoon. Happy?"

"Not entirely. I want in."

"In?"

"I want out of this tank, and you're my ticket."

"I'm *so* curious why you think I'd agree to that."

"You're weak. Far too weak to pull this off. You're pretending to have forgiven the priest, even in the absence of his contrition. Maybe you think this sets you on a moral high ground, but you'd be deluded in that case. You are, in fact, sitting on a wound, and within that wound is the energy required to pass over. But you're too afraid to face that, because you might discover a well of hatred so deep it would consume you. You're not ready to deal with murderous rage, the kind so ferocious it tilts toward madness. I get that. I do. Who would *want* to look into that mirror? So if you're going to pass over, you'll need my help. I can give you the necessary boost."

"Even if that were true—*if* it were—what would you get in return?"

"I get to leave with you. I escape this tank. I witness your haunting, and, if possible, help. Maybe I even secure my own passing over. Who knows."

"No one knows, right?"

"Bingo, kid."

Álvaro shook his head and pursed his lips. "Ok, Ricky. Álvaro. My name is Álvaro Bandono."

A grin spread across Ricky's face. "Al Bandono, huh."

"I don't go by Al."

"A…bandono."

"…Yes."

"Almost as if you were destined to be *a*…bandoned." Ricky guffawed.

"You done?" said Álvaro.

"Just gettin' started. Man alive! You're a hoot."

"Let's get moving."

"Go on, then. Concentrate that will."

So Álvaro did.

With their combined spiritual energy, Álvaro and Ricky found a path out of the water tank and through the pipes. They surfaced in a toilet bowl full of fetid feces, dark urine, and disintegrating toilet paper. Someone had forgotten to flush the toilet in the staff bathroom.

"Well done, kid."

"Don't be sarcastic. I did what you said. I concentrated."

"I'm not squeezin' your cheese. You did good."

"Then why are we in this soiled toilet…where's the priest?"

"All in good time. We're out of the tank and into the toilet bowl. Movement is good."

"But movement where?"

"Stay calm. Concentrate, and another step will present itself."

"How am I supposed to concentrate when I'm floating in excrement?"

"Did I tell you this would be easy? Who promised

you that? You Americans think life is a Tom Cruise action movie with a Diane Keaton romcom happy ending. Entitled. Historical amnesiacs. Naive optimists. Trigger-happy monkeys. Ach, it makes me sick."

"Well, howdy *doody*. Anything else you need to get off your chest, Ricky? I'm Mexican, by the way. I only grew up in the States. Besides, you sound American, too."

"German. I went to the American school in Berlin before moving here. Where I met Sally Jenkins, you may remember. I also watched a lot of *Friends*."

The bathroom door flung open. Footsteps squeaked across the tile. In a hurry, the janitor slipped into the stall and locked it. He undid his drawers.

"Oh God."

"Yes," said Ricky.

"We've got to get out of here."

"Don't give up now."

"He didn't even flush the leftovers. This guy is desperate. He's going to dump another load."

"Yes," said Ricky, steeling himself. "Yes, he is."

The janitor threw his drawers to the floor. His rump was neither young nor beautiful. Down came that hairy saggy butthole.

"Run!" screamed Álvaro. "Back down the pipe."

"Hold the line."

"Come on!"

"Hooooold."

"Oh no. No no no no…"

"Hold!"

"God help us."

"If it's sufficiently runny, we can travel the flow into the janitor."

"*What?*"

"I feel a growing sense of control. We can choose the path now."

"Even if we could control our trajectory, why would we go *inside?*"

"He'll cross paths with the priest at some point."

"It could be days or weeks."

"We have no choice. The time to shovel your own shit has come. Set your aim. Will it!"

"Not like this…"

Undigested chilis, Chinese mushrooms, and tiny corns fell like a hailstorm. The janitor had eaten a level-ten spicy entrée at a Sichuan restaurant the night before.

"I see the opening. The energy is right. Now. Now!" yelled Ricky, leaping into the flow.

"No!"

"Hurry!" screamed Ricky, disappearing into the janitor's bum.

Álvaro closed his eyes and willed himself into the jet stream. Luckily, it was so runny that he swam like a trout, upstream into the colon, where Ricky pulled him into the bloodstream, through the heart, and up to the eyes.

"We've leveled up. Can you feel it? We have agency," said Ricky.

"I have vertigo."

"Relax. Take a moment."

Álvaro did. Then he looked around and said: "I don't get it. Where's this guy's spirit?"

"Whose?"

"The janitor's. Shouldn't someone be upset that we barged in like this?"

"This guy? You nuts? How do you think Father Forbidden Fellatio gets away with it? The janitor is empty, a completely vacant soul. He sees all the clues, of course.

The cameras in the rafters. The change in the kids' behavior. He notices the small details like any housekeeper does. And he chooses to do nothing."

"How can that be?"

"Jiminy Cricket's crotch, you're naive! It's in his self-interest. The priest pays. And better than most, oddly enough. Where else would this snaggle-toothed nincompoop find employment?"

"Isn't that a bit harsh?"

"For the guy who turned a blind eye while you were raped."

"Right."

"Wake up you wimpy wide-eyed willow wisp. It's time to accept that this wild world is full of wickedness, especially on the spirit side. So keep your tits about you."

"Wits."

"What I said. Keep your wits near your tits."

"My wits are near this guy's man tits. Does that count?"

"A joke! Atta boy! Aye, that counts."

Once the worst of the initial dump had passed, the janitor released a sigh of extreme exhaustion. He pulled out his phone. The screen came alive with vibrant colors.

"Fortune favors the bold!" exclaimed Ricky.

"We've been bold enough for ten lifetimes."

"Ten lifetimes? *Life*times? We're living spirits *beyond time*. Eternity awaits, you bastard's son of a dingleberry! Onward ho!"

Álvaro groaned, and Ricky grinned.

"Cheer up. This is going to be fun. We're about to digitize."

"Digitize?"

The janitor's fingers tapped a mazerunner game.

"Spirits flow well through water, obviously. We always knew that. But as you learned while zipping under the altar, electricity really *really* works. So what does that mean?"

"There's no electrical connection here to ride."

"Radiation, kid. Electromagnetic radiation. Time to surf the spiritual highway."

"Surf?"

"The radio frequencies are calling me."

"I don't know."

"Pack your shit, Dorothy. We're leaving Kansas and going way past Wonderland."

"You mean Alice."

"I mean Álvaro. Get ready to move your ass."

"I'm ready."

"You damn well better be. EMR is to a spirit what the Roman road was to the chariot."

"You have no idea what you're talking about."

"God Bless the sexually frustrated technonerds who put one of these ever-emitting phones into every pocket from Bangalore to Budapest, Brooklyn to Beijing, Boca Raton to Bumbumba...."

"Stop making love to your own voice, and get on with it."

"Style, my boy. Style! Flare! Beauty! Form!"

The janitor closed the maze runner app and slipped the phone inside his pocket.

"All your blabber, and we've missed our chance."

"O ye of little faith."

Through the janitor's jeans, signal after signal escaped. Ricky identified an incoming radio wave and catapulted their spirits into the phone, whose screen was dark. They couldn't see a thing.

"Ow!"

"Move out of the way."

"Ow! Jesus!"

"Well, *move!*"

"Follow me," said Ricky.

They bumped in and out of alleyways between home screen applications until Ricky found the Settings icon. He spent some time acquainting himself with the available networks while Álvaro shivered in the dark.

Eventually, Ricky identified the church's WiFi. It was unlocked, so they hopped effortlessly to the central router, which was located atop a set of drawers in the priest's office.

"Look familiar?" asked Ricky.

Álvaro shook with pain and terror.

Many incidents that led up to the rape had occurred in this very room, a rather typical administrative office in a church. Linoleum floors, square tile ceiling, long white tube lights. A leather chair on rollers behind a cheap desk. Near the window, a small couch and coffee table. A fake hibiscus tree in a lonely corner. On the white wall hung a solitary wooden cross. Christ was there, too.

"Let it out," said Ricky, patting Álvaro's shoulder as he shook off the panic attack.

Álvaro sniffled and settled down.

Only for a moment.

The priest walked in. His hair had grayed, and wrinkles rippled across his forehead. He'd developed a bit of a floppy neck, too. Same clerical get-up, though.

"Okay, kid," said Ricky. "Time to focus. Just..."

"Shut up," said Ál, terse with rage.

For once, Ricky obeyed.

Moments later, the lights flickered. On and off in several bursts, like triplets. The priest looked up from his desk, waited for the lights to revert to normal, and returned his work.

"You're a natural, kid. Classic horror film flickering lights."

"I need more."

Álvaro remembered the priest's touch. He remembered the taste of his semen and the satisfied twinkle in the man's eyes. He smelled the salty sweat and felt the priest's slimy seed inside him. These memories boiled over in a stew of contempt that Álvaro directed toward the lights. On and off again they came in bursts, settling in the off position.

The priest sighed and stood. He approached and flicked the switch on. Then off. Then on. He proved to himself that it still worked. He felt no fear. No confusion. No doubt. He assumed the circuit needed replaced. He had not a single thought of the supernatural.

"It's not working," said Álvaro.

"Give it time."

"I'm spent."

"You done good for one day. We should head back into the Wi-Fi router."

"Why?"

"Can't you feel it? There's energy emanating closer to the source. It'll charge us up."

The next day, an HVAC technician finished installing a smart thermostat throughout the church. They had finally found the funds to modernize.

Álvaro, buzzing with spiritual energy, used this vast new network to visit every room in the administrative offices and most of the chapel. He bounced happily along their Wi-Fi interconnectedness like a frog across lily pads.

A burst of creativity followed this exploration, and with abundant joy, he returned to the office eager to enact novel haunting techniques.

"I'm gonna haunt the Hell out of him, Ricky!"

Ricky didn't answer. He was staring out the window with a glazed, confused look. Overnight, while Álvaro gained energy, Ricky had lost it. Something about his proximity to the source produced the exact opposite effect, and he had slumped into a depression.

"Ricky?"

"Huh? Oh, hey kid."

"You alright?"

Ricky laughed and roused himself. "Sure. Yeah. Just savoring the sunrise. Smelling the shastas. Singing the songs I like to sing. What's up?"

"I'm ready to haunt. Big time."

"That's great. Good stuff."

"I'm gonna haunt the Hell out of him."

Ricky chuckled and pat Álvaro on the shoulder.

"Haunt it *into* him, kid."

In walked the priest. He carried a thin leather briefcase and a large Starbucks cup, which he sipped gingerly and savored with orgasmic relish.

Álvaro perked up at the sight, emboldened by his plans.

The priest turned on his laptop, and Álvaro leapt inside and started sniffing around.

Sniff sniff sniff.

Buried within the priest's archives was a trove of video files. The man had far too much pride to allow the beauty of his treachery to fall victim to impermanence. Future generations must know what he'd accomplished.

Álvaro was keen to help.

At the speed of light, for that's what Álvaro's supercharged spirit had effectively become, he reviewed the hundreds of videos that recorded indecent acts in all their savage cruelty. Not only had the priest filmed himself and his altar boys. He had also, on multiple occasions, recruited a priest from a neighboring parish. And once, even, a bishop. Most shots were recorded from above the altar, way way on high. The video quality was 4K, maybe higher. What money they must have spent hanging those cameras! And what lies they must have told during installation.

Álvaro copied the files and transferred them to the front office secretary's old desktop tower, which was always turned on and tapped into the Wi-Fi. It was a most handy storage and distribution center.

Then he zoomed back to Ricky at the router.

"Ready to laugh so hard you'll cry like Mary on the Mount?"

"Jesus, kid. What happened to bitching about blaspheming?"

"I'm a new man."

Álvaro grinned, and Ricky shook his head.

While Fickoft was answering a slew of Easter-related emails (that day was the Saturday before Easter Sunday), a full-screen pop-up appeared on his laptop. It was blank and contained no option to minimize. No 'x' to click. No luck with control+alt+M, either. The whole screen was a big black empty box with a gray border.

The priest scratched his head. He sucked his teeth. He

shifted in his chair. He reached to pick up the phone for tech support.

Text appeared on screen:

I like the way you sin. —The Holy Ghost.

The priest furrowed his brow.

A video began.

There he was, decades back, penetrating his most beloved altar boy, Álvaro. The sound came on, sending moans out the office's open door. Blood rushed to Fickoft's face as he jammed a finger on the mute button. No effect. He ran to the door and slammed it shut.

Inside the router, Álvaro looked at Ricky.

"How about it, huh? Pretty slick?"

"Inspired, kid."

Álvaro was too excited to notice Ricky's deflated tone.

When the laptop wouldn't shut off, Fickoft considered throwing it out the window or smashing it. Instead, he placed the computer in his briefcase, which he then wrapped in a thick woolen coat. Finally, he locked that bundle in the closet and scurried to the bathroom.

No more moans. Blessed silence.

Álvaro grabbed Ricky, and they zipped via Wi-Fi into the priest's phone.

Hyperventilating, Fickoft locked himself in a bathroom stall and knelt before the toilet, prepared to vomit. When nothing came up, he flipped down the lid and sat, awaiting the other option. Down and out. Something had to give. The nausea was overwhelming.

But nothing happened. So he performed a breathing exercise to calm his heartrate.

Fickoft pulled out his phone and opened the bishop's contact card. He had to alert his accomplice. They were compromised. But the number never appeared. Instead, a video of the priest and the bishop double-teaming another boy popped up.

The priest shrieked and dropped the phone into the toilet bowl.

Álvaro cackled like a hyena.

Seconds before the phone fried from water damage, they transferred to the nearest smart thermostat, then back to the router, and finally, into the navigation console of the priest's Mercedes-Benz, parked right outside the office.

The holy man was soon speeding home in desperation. Álvaro held back on haunting in traffic. Too risky. He didn't want to kill his victim before justice had been served.

Once Fickoft parked in the driveway, Álvaro put yet another video on the console. The priest bashed the screen until its crystals were an indecipherable mash of colors. He ran inside and locked the deadbolt, as if that might save him.

But Álvaro and Ricky were too strong. They broke the password for his home Wi-Fi and let themselves in.

For the rest of that Saturday, Álvaro tortured the priest's conscience. He played select audio excerpts from the rapes on surround sound, drawing the priest's attention to nearby empty rooms. Behind him. Then in front. Downstairs. Upstairs. All around, all at once. Often just loudly enough to make the holy man doubt whether he'd heard any noise at all. Or perhaps all of this was in his mind? Could guilt *really* be as strong as his parishioners had always complained?

The priest came to suspect his own incipient madness. To avoid a complete unraveling, he took sleeping pills. At least there, perhaps, he could not be tormented. And when he woke? He would pray for peace, silence, and amnesia.

None came.

In the wee hours of Easter Sunday, the priest's living room TV burst on with volume at full blast. Wailing, weeping. Slapping. Moans of pleasure. Dirty talk of the foulest kind.

Fickoft ran downstairs and ripped it off the wall.

Sweating and mumbling, he dressed in his robe and drove to the cathedral, which, although fully prepped for Easter mass, was mercifully empty. He shuddered at the sight of the cross over the altar and crept away, hunched in shame and frantic with terror. He locked himself in the confessional and prayed for mercy. He ran rosary beads through his fingers. He chanted.

Pie Jesu Domine, vocame cum benedictis, quam olim Abrahae promisisti.

"Promisisti!" he shouted.

Parishioners arrived. Soon, the church was packed, and he was trapped inside. It wasn't a normal crowd either. Rather, an Easter Sunday crowd. The programme was in four languages: English, Spanish, Haitian Creole, and Vietnamese. Extra pews had been sent for. Two choirs had been assembled. There was even an above-ground, blow-up pool near the pulpit for adult baptisms.

Today was the day of their Lord, and for many, an induction into the faith.

The priest managed to sneak off to the bathroom, calm his nerves, and set a winning Sunday smile on his face. He delivered his sermon, knees shaking under his robe. But he kept a straight enough face. Regulars noticed that his delivery was flat. Or off in some way. Newcomers figured he was another boring lecturer who clung desperately to notes.

After the homily, Fickoft settled next to the choir, closed his eyes, and prayed.

The ushers passed donation plates down the pews.

"Donations are now also accepted through our app," explained a deacon.

"Please use the QR code found in your church bulletin."

About halfway down in pew number four sat a particularly devoted parishioner: sweet little crinkly old pious Grandma Jibberjabber. She was a stunning ninety-eight year-old relic who, out of a deep fear of mugging, had ceased to carry cash. She had also, through herculean personal effort and painstaking assistance from both her grandsons, recently learned to use the aforementioned QR code. Granny Jibjab — as the children's choir called her — removed a smart phone from her mint green purse and held it precariously beneath her clouded triple-thick lenses. The screen tilted back and forth as her wrist, supported so feebly by ever-weakening muscles, shook with a concert violinist's vibrato. But Jibbyjabby was prayerful, patient, and strong with the Lord, who provided just enough strength to that ancient wrist such that, by golly, she was the first in the whole congregation to navigate to the website linked in the QR Code.

She was also the first (and only, thankfully) to drop dead upon sight of its contents.

Screams of horror and enraged shouts erupted in the church. Devout women fainted. Children cried. Nuns crossed themselves. Other visiting holy men went as pale as their collared inserts. Some pews emptied toward the back. Others, angrier ones, marched toward the pulpit.

Cries of "Bastard! My boy wasn't lying! Pervert!

Liar!" drowned all else.

Anyone who'd attempted a digital donation instead saw a video of the priest in action.

Álvaro, from his perch in one of the ceiling cams, watched with pleasure as the mass came undone, a process capstoned by the spilling of the baptismal pool and subsequent flooding of the church's plumbing.

He poked Ricky.

"You're missing it!"

Ricky had lost so much energy, he couldn't even keep his eyes open.

"They're horrified. My God, Ricky look at the rage, the disillusionment, the pain!"

"You enjoy, kid. I've lost my appetite."

"Come on. This is the ultimate justice. It's hilarious. The dark comic truth, revealed!"

Ricky shook his head.

"What?" said Álvaro, annoyed. "Suddenly, God doesn't find this suffering hilarious?"

"Maybe He never did."

"You're so full of shit."

Ricky made his six shooters. *Pow pow pow.* But with lazy movements. He managed to open his eyes. They were weary and filled with sorrow.

"Bingo. It's all lies. Welcome to the Shit Parade."

"No, *you* are all lies. That," Álvaro pointed toward the cathedral scene, "that is real. That man destroyed my life. Now everyone can see him as he *truly* is."

"Hah."

"What?" Álvaro was pissed now. "Funny again?"

"You had your faith when you met me. Do you have it now?"

"Of course. Nothing's changed."

"Those people. Their hearts won't survive it."

"That's on God."

"Not you?"

"What am I but an instrument?"

"Bravo, kid. You've finally arrived."

"Go to Hell."

"Bought my ticket a long time ago."

Ricky closed his eyes and felt himself fading. Fading and falling, all the way down into the hot water tank.

Álvaro continued to admire his handiwork, and for a while, he was most satisfied. Fickoft went catatonic and was escorted out in handcuffs. The second-in-command, fresh from seminary, overcame his immediate shock and stepped in as shepherd of the flock. Within an hour, he had restored order and contacted a bishop (not *that* bishop) who contacted a cardinal.

And so on.

Fulfilled and triumphant, Álvaro floated among the gothic arches, riding the Wi-Fi signals as they bounced around. He'd completed his haunting and yearned to cross over. But the day ended, and nothing happened. Then a week passed, and nothing still. Endless spiritual time flowed, yet he neither ascended to Heaven nor descended into Hell. He remained in the cathedral, slowly losing energy, until one day he found himself in the hot water tank, side by side with Ricky.

Back down in that problem plumbing.

"I don't know what to tell you, kid."

"It's okay," said Álvaro.

"I really thought we were getting out of here."

"I know."

"I saw others move on."

"Yeah."

"I promise you. I felt them cross over."
"I believe you."
"Yeah?"
"Yeah."
"Then why do you sound do down?"
"I'm waiting for you to cheer me up."

Marketplace of Sin

Three months after her father threw himself from a bridge, seventeen-year-old Lucy Zauberbruck found an eviction notice on the kitchen counter. In a panic, she marched through the tiny, dingy apartment and presented the notice to her mother, who, clad in a wrinkled sweatsuit, lay prostrate sipping red wine and watching game shows.

"Don't cry now."

"Why haven't you paid?"

"Do *you* have money?"

"What about the insurance?"

Her mother rolled her eyes.

"Dad's note said…"

"Grow up, Lucy. The loser killed himself. Suicide doesn't pay."

Lucy rode the bus up the hill to the wealthy neighborhood, where she babysat two children for a lovely couple who owned a large, luxurious home.

That's where she found the necklace.

While playing hide and seek, one of the kids went missing. Lucy and the younger sister scoured the in-bounds area: the family room, the kitchen, the garage, the kids' bedrooms.

"It's not funny!" the little girl whined.

Lucy called the older brother's name and threatened severe punishment. Nothing.

Out-of-bounds, then.

As soon as they entered the master bedroom, the boy leapt out of the closet, howling with laughter. His sister frolicked after him, and they ran downstairs. Only Lucy remained, worried about the pile of socks and underwear that had fallen out of the closet.

Lucy folded each piece to approximate the original arrangement.

That's when she saw it.

A slender white box had tumbled open, revealing a gold necklace with shimmering diamonds. For a moment, Lucy was breathless, overwhelmed by the beauty. Then she noticed the card. *To Cecilia, my little minx.* Signed by the husband. Cecilia was the maid.

Scumbag, thought Lucy.

Later that night, the couple bickered bitterly as they walked in.

"Are you in love?"

"For Christ's sake!"

"I saw how you looked at her."

"Honey, *please.*"

A door slammed. The garage door shook.

Lucy needed to catch the last bus. She waited as long as possible before entering the kitchen.

The mother sat on a stool, bleeding mascara.

"Oh," she said with a sorrowful smile. "Here."

She slipped far too much money into Lucy's hand and shooed her out the door.

Lucy was stunned. Each step toward the bus was a relief. Perhaps she would never need to explain the boy or the closet. Perhaps she could even forget the necklace. But no, the husband's infidelity had shaken her. That such a loving family might come undone was one tragedy too many.

Lucy rode the bus down into the valley, to the poor part of town. As always, she enjoyed the final Christmas gift her father had given her: high-quality, over-ear headphones. She blasted sneaky, freaky, brutal, demented metal, the darkest genre she knew.

As the music played, an idea presented itself: steal the necklace.

Pawn it. Pay the rent. Shame the husband. Save the marriage.

The next day after school, as she'd done every day since his death, Lucy went to the bridge to speak with her father. It was a foggy evening, and the pedestrian walk was deserted. Two crows perched on a stone pillar whose foundation plunged into the murky river.

"I wish you were here, Dad."

The crows cawed, and the fog lifted, revealing a rusted gate and staircase.

Fearful yet curious, Lucy descended the stairs and heard a quirky melody that beckoned her onto a platform at the river's edge.

"Not even a nibble," grumbled a shadow in the fog.

A tall, bulky figure stepped out. He wore a navy overcoat, a sailor's cap, and held a fishing rod. His round, lumpy face had a snub nose, and one eye was drastically larger than the other.

"Was that you making music?" Lucy asked.

"Music," he said, incredulous. "An humble troll couldn't...and yet..."

"Troll, huh? Well, I swear I heard some. Are you alone?"

"None more alone than me. Nix, they call me."

"Nix?"

"Nix, some say. Nought say others. Nothing, you may also call me."

"Hello, Nix. I've never seen this staircase before."

"You weren't looking, miss. But Nix is always here to do his duty!"

"And what's that?"

Nix snarled. "Unclear! Muddied are the waters, and rusted is the bridge. There be my boat, sunk against the mooring. I used to ferry passengers. Then up went the bridge, and you being a clever gal must know…"

"Trolls guard bridges."

"Yes, yes! Nix preferred the freedom of the boat. Now I oversee this bridge, and if you make a deal with me, I will permit your crossing. "

"I don't want to cross. I came to speak with my father."

"Miss, your father is with the river."

This terrified Lucy. "How do you know he's dead?"

"Of Death Nix knows nothing. No, no! One might say, rather, the river speaks for him."

"Then I should speak to the river."

"Clever, indeed! But you are not ready. Too young and vulnerable."

"I'm tougher than you think."

"Even so! Better to cross."

"How can I trust you?"

Nix's eyes twinkled. "You cannot! No trust under the bridge. Only faith and doubt."

"Is this some sort of riddle?"

"An offer, miss," he said. "A special offer, one unlike any other I have made, for you have awoken a desire in me. Yes, yes! A very un-troll-like desire."

Lucy bit her lip and looked back at the stairs. They'd disappeared.

"Well, go on."

"To cross, you must give me your sin."

"Who says I have any sin?"

"I see one growing in your heart."

"The necklace."

"Yes, yes! This I greatly desire."

"Why?"

"A sin committed in innocent desperation, aimed with good intentions…a most valuable prize! Yes, yes! For this, the barge master might even trade his magic flute."

"If I agree, what happens?"

"The sin will be erased."

"Erased?"

"You will not steal the necklace."

"And the rent? The family?"

"Any problems which your sin would have sought to address shall be resolved."

"Resolved…how?"

"Not for Nix, Nought, Nothing to say, miss."

"So that's the catch."

Nix grinned. "Fisherman as I am, there must be a catch."

Lucy barely gave it thought. Better to risk this than face certain eviction and despair.

"I accept."

Nix danced a little jig.

"How do I…?"

"Close your eyes, and pray that you pass on this sin."

Lucy did as instructed.

Nix dug into one of the many pockets of his jacket's inner lining and procured a red feathery lure labeled LUST. He admired it, affixed it, and cast the line into the river.

When Lucy opened her eyes, Nix was straining to reel in his catch. Triumphantly, he thrust his shoulders back and revealed the prize: a necklace identical in form to the father's purchase, but its diamonds were black.

Nix unhooked the necklace, and the earth shook.

Lucy ducked for cover as a stone fell from the pillar into the river.

"Grumble away, entitled spirits!" Nix bellowed, shaking a fist. "Old Nix feels a flute solo coming on!"

Then Nix laughed such a deep, wild laugh that Lucy fell right asleep.

The following morning, Lucy awoke with a memory of the troll like a dream. She received a voicemail from the father, asking if she was available that night. For the last minute request, he offered double.

More money. Was Nix *real*?

After school, Lucy thought of her father but felt no desire to visit the bridge. Bitter grief had calmed to quiet pain. In the apartment, her mother was asleep, an empty glass at her side. Lucy sniffed it. Water. She checked the cabinets. Empty of wine. The kitchen was clean, and on the counter was a check from her aunt.

After everything, they'd made up?

So much money, so little time.

With skeptical optimism, Lucy boarded the bus and slid on her headphones. The music application suggested a release from a peculiar debut artist.

Lucy gawked.

The album cover showed Nix in a medieval jester's costume: hat, slippers, the whole shebang. He was climbing into a cave, one foot inside. He grinned mischievously and held a gnarled finger to his lips—*shhh*. The music itself was comical, impish rock, to which Lucy couldn't help but tap her feet.

Where's the flute solo? she wondered

The father answered the door in a handsome maroon suit, leather loafers, and a musky cologne that sent tingles down Lucy's spine.

"Hurry up, hun!" hollered the wife, playfully.

She waltzed into the foyer in a tight black slip and nuzzled her husband's neck.

Lucy's mouth hung agape.

Not only was their fight over, the mother was smitten.

"We'll be back by eleven," the father said.

As instructed, Lucy ordered pizza, which the kids devoured in front of the TV. She put on their favorite episode of their favorite cartoon. Barring a housefire, they would not turn away.

Lucy went upstairs. Alone.

In the master bedroom, she snuck her hand under the clothes pile in the closet and found the jewelry box. The same as before, but inside was the necklace that had been fished out of the river. Black diamonds. She hunched over and stared, ensnared by its terrible, pure beauty.

Lucy heard the children howl with laughter downstairs. She snapped out of her daze and set the room as it had been.

When the parents returned, they were tipsy. Lucy had no trouble hiding her guilt for snooping in the bedroom. She gave her nightly report and got paid.

On the bus down, another album dropped. This one showed Nix as a humanoid spermatozoon in the center of an egg-like Earth, gleefully pulling levers as a volcano erupted on the surface. The music was the deepest, darkest, industrial techno she'd ever heard, as if each thunderous beat were the tectonic pounding of pistons from a gruesome, magnificent machine.

Lucy listened while brooding on the necklace.

Soon, she felt slimy and aroused.

The next morning, Lucy received another voicemail from the father. More work. This time, she didn't think about money or magic. Rather, she devised a plan to spend even more time with the necklace.

On the ascent, another album dropped. The cover depicted Nix in booty shorts and a crop top, dangling his legs from an asteroid, fishing with a flute as a rod, cast in a river of space dust. The music, a manically happy electropop, was so demanding that Lucy bounced in her seat until her armpits were sweaty.

Still no flute solo, though.

The second the couple left, Lucy crushed sleeping pills into the children's applesauce. They were soon yawning under the covers.

In the master bathroom, Lucy stripped and lay the necklace across her bare chest. She gazed into the mirror with such intense pleasure that, much to her surprise, the reflection grinned back. It rubbed the necklace, as if the gold chain might be aroused, and the metal melted like butter in a pan.

Lucy watched, helpless and immobile, as gold slowly covered her breasts in the mirror.

The garage door rattled.

The parents were home.

Panicked, Lucy dressed, covered her tracks, and jumped onto the couch downstairs, sweaty with fear. Her heart thumped wildly. Surely, the wife would sense violation this time.

But the husband returned home alone. One of the couple's recently divorced friends, he explained, had been desperate to find a guy, so his wife stayed out to wingwoman.

Lucy noticed the husband's firm muscles and stubbled jawline as if for the first time.

She took the money and ran, panting.

Outside, the dense fog from the bridge had found its way atop the hill. When Lucy reached the sidewalk, a flute solo caught her ear. Terrified, she whirled around and watched the fog retreat.

The house's stone turret had taken the form of a golden human breast, to which Nix clung, swaddled in a cloth diaper. He sucked on the tip like a nipple. From the flute-shaped chimney soared his jazzy, virtuosic solo.

Lucy's hips swayed, bouncing between revulsion and desire like a metronome.

The solo faded out, and with it the fog and the vision.

Lucy felt herself fading, too. Skin, then muscles, then bone, until only half of her spirit remained. There was no pain. Only awareness that she had become her mirror image.

The husband opened the door.

"Lucy?"

"Bring me my necklace, slave."

In the Devil's Sock Drawer

The morning after my botched double mastectomy, I fall out of bed and tumble into the Devil's sock drawer. It is messy as Hell. Bones and petrified organs and ligaments are scattered among piles of socks, each woven from the lives of countless cursed souls. I've never been somewhere so strange, and, as if by some malevolent static electricity, my arm hairs stand on end. My heart races, and I wonder how this all got here, how I got here, and why am I wearing running shoes?

But, if there is some chaotic, necessary design lurking within this place, I don't want to understand. No, rather, I *shouldn't* understand.

I take a deep breath and think.

Death comes to mind.

Is that because I'm down *here*?

I'm a queasy sort, no question. But death never used to frighten me. For instance, I vomited in my mouth when the surgeon told me he would remove my breasts, starting with a small incision below the left nipple. Then another below the right. On the other hand, I didn't worry about chemotherapy and a slow, withering death. Maybe that's because I never expected to find myself here, in the Devil's sock drawer.

Something tells me that death—slow and withering or sudden and final—hides in every corner of this place.

Maybe not. Maybe I'm exaggerating a new fear.

I guess I'll say a prayer.

Cross my fingers, too. Can't hurt...

I need a plan, so I assess my physical situation. I'm the size of a tiny figurine down here, and the piles of socks are stacked in enormous, orderly columns like inside an ancient Egyptian temple. The area is lit by crackling torches whose golden sconces resemble cuff links, loose buttons, and tuxedo studs. A harmony of whispers—faint, dissonant, and pleading—leaks from the columns. It's all too surreal to determine a clear, meaningful direction. So, curious like a god of the underworld, I take my first step on pure impulse. I press my ear against a black and red striped dress sock.

"Overstay and fray," it says.

I touch the silk fabric, and a white athletic sock beckons.

"If you fray, don't stray."

A bright white light suddenly blinds me, then fades to a single point at the back of the drawer, where it originated.

"Look ahead, not up," counsels a gray wool sock.

I peek around nearby columns, searching for similar lights, but this is the only one of its kind. Though I feel a warning in my heart, I am compelled to seek its source. Perhaps, I hope, it is a way out. Whatever it *may be* is irrelevant.

I set off running.

"Beware," squeaks a baby lavender sock.

"Beware the Strings of Fate!"

I keep a brisk pace and crunch bones underfoot. The air is surprisingly clean and oxygen-rich. My muscles strain and stretch. Despite the glowing torches, I cannot discern the distance to the light, which is nothing more than a pinpoint through the colonnade. The length of my journey is uncertain, and the path through the columns winds unpredictably. Each row of columns I pass is evenly spaced, meticulously piled, and identical, such that I perceive no progress, even as I feel my body's exertions.

Am I running in circles?

Perhaps, but I am too desperate to doubt the instinct that propels me.

Once my knees start to ache, I realize I have closed the gap. By what distance? In what time? Impossible to measure. Pain is the only certainty.

My body is hot and sweaty but not too tired, and the Devil's sock drawer is finally changing. The air has become damp and smells of moldy feet. The columns in this section are in disrepair: sock heels worn through, elastic welts ripped to scraggly ends. They beg me to stop and snip, to prune their neglected strands and ease their unraveling.

But I resist temptation in this dark place. There are no more sconces or torches. Only dim heaps of embers at each column's base, like campfires hastily abandoned. Clouds of sparks float in the air, threatening to catch.

I am in great danger.

To stop here, even for a moment, could be fatal.

I run and run until my hip joints are inflamed and grinding. I feel a surge of hope as I notice the white light has grown larger and brighter. But in this final stretch, fatigue seeps into my bones. The sock columns are a jungle of frayed fibers, towering like abandoned skyscrapers smothered by vines. Dangling, multicolored threads brush against my head and shoulders from above. Do they hang from a ceiling whose weight the columns support? I am tempted to glance upward, but I remember the counsel of the gray wool sock.

Look ahead, not up.

I focus on the light, which has taken the shape of a keyhole.

My posture starts to fail, shoulders slumping, chest caving inward. The air is hot and humid, a suffocating smog dense with airborne fungi.

Am I soon to meet the Devil?

I pant and cough, slackening my pace. I notice I'm fraying, too. At first, it seems my forearm hair is once again standing on end. Is it the malevolent static electricity? On closer inspection, I see my skin is unraveling in a precise, methodical fashion. Layer by layer, my hands disassemble: skin, muscles, ligaments, bones, and fluids, down to the cellular and molecular levels. Finally, a double helix of my DNA uncrosses itself like a solved Cat's Cradle, revealing the two strings of my soul. One vanishes slowly, like the last wisp of smoke from a burnt effigy. In its absence, I feel my heart break, filling this lonely drawer with that much more pain. The remaining string hovers, balanced in the palm of what used to be my hand. I am mesmerized by its form, color, and brilliance. So mesmerized, in fact, that I slide into a blissful oblivion where I forget my pain and nearly everything else. When I come to, I look for the familiar columns. Perhaps I may find another wool sock woven with wisdom, one of a different color than gray.

But there are no more columns.

I have reached the back of the Devil's sock drawer.

As I approach the keyhole, my remaining soul string starts to dance, bouncing toward the ceiling with no particular training or purpose. Just dancing, as far as I can tell. Or perhaps it's being pulled by a force, one that, if I could pass through here again, I'd risk my life to glimpse. But there's no time or energy left. The rest of my body is unraveling, and I collapse before the light, which disappears.

What appears in its place? A simple corner of a drawer. The smooth edge along which two walls meet. Nothing more.

What hope I had melts into disillusion. I place my head in what's left of my hands and cry.

The only source of light is a pale gray aura, which shines from above.

In the empty corner of the Devil's sock drawer, I lie on my back. The Strings of Fate hang from above, teasing the tip of my ticklish nose, giving me the giggles. Suddenly, I feel a force—perhaps the one that choreographs my string— tugging on my vocal cords. It drags my esophagus and lungs and guts and genitals skyward in one long, continuous flow. I let them go freely and feel an extraordinary weightlessness, as if I am become the String of my Fate. A brilliant, colorful, dancing, vibrating, shimmying thing—nothing profound, nothing sacred— just an object animated by forces with which it has come to terms.

Ever since I took my tumble, I have tasted nothing. Not even the sweat on my upper lip. I've felt neither hunger nor thirst. Curious, given my extreme physical effort to reach the light. Perhaps I am too filled with disgust at the stubborn memory of my botched surgery. What's more, I haven't felt any sexual desire down here. Could this also be a product of disgust? No, I would have needed to run into some*body* to feel sexual desire. All I've seen are strings, and there's nothing arousing about a string.

Probably.

Not that any of those concerns are relevant to my current *physical* situation. I'm no longer a body. I've been stripped bare to my simple lonely string. Even if I were served a sizzling steak of the finest grass-fed beef slaughtered with dignity, I couldn't taste it if wanted to. Not anymore than I could touch, see, smell, or hear it.

Still, as senseless as I am, I open a new sense. What is its nature? I cannot be sure. But with this sense, I perceive a presence in the pale glow. Up *there.* It is looking down, staring into my dancing string.

Terror kills my vibe.

A ten-limbed spider has nested in the nothingness of the back corner of the Devil's sock drawer. It collects my soul on a spool, winding me round and round, like the indifferent, ticking hands of a clock. Eight hairy legs stabilize its gargantuan black body on a labyrinthine web, while a pair of human hands deftly work a shiny silver loom.

I recognize the spider's many eyes: my own.

"I didn't expect to find you down here," I say.

"What makes you think I'm down there?" it asks, scuttling up through the ceiling.

Cold Hard Love

On a cold, cloudy Valentine's Day at West Youghiogheny High School, Chris Rittermacher got caught giving Paul Czernak a blowjob. The young men left their respective classes halfway through second period, met in the auditorium bathroom (the most deserted), smoked weed from Paul's bubbler (exhaling out the window), and got to business. It was their first attempt at such clandestine activity, and it might have worked out seamlessly, were it not for vice-principal Conrad Butterhalter.

For months, Butterhalter had been struggling with his prostate, and after a backstage meeting with the band director, he was forced to make an irregular stop in the auditorium bathroom. He hesitated to use a student lavatory, but desperate times called for desperate measures. He'd only just unzipped his fly when he smelled the smoke.

"Nothing I can do about pot in the parking lot," Butterhalter whispered, zipping up.

He checked under the stalls.

"But in here…in here you are mine."

He saw knees on the ground next to a toilet and banged a fist against the stall door.

"Open up," he commanded.

There was a spit, a plop, and a flush.

"Now!"

The door opened.

"Czernak," Butterhalter muttered. "Again."

He lifted the other student's baby-faced chin.

"Christopher Rittermacher…"

The shock and disappointment in Butterhalter's voice overwhelmed Chris, who'd never been in trouble. Not once. Not with his parents, not with a teacher. Certainly not a school administrator.

Chris was so distraught, he could barely breath as he waddled head down to Butterhalter's office.

But Chris had other problems on his mind: his alcoholic, homophobic father; his devout Christian mother; and perhaps worst of all, his girlfriend, with whom he'd made tender love only days before.

None of them knew Chris was gay.

Meanwhile, Joe Rittermacher, Chris's older brother, stopped at Ribeye's Deli to buy Valentine's Day roses for his mother. He had no girlfriend to buy for, and he knew his inconsiderate father wasn't going to get anything.

On his way to the registers, Joe passed the butcher and saw a suggestive package in the display case: 'Valentine's Day Meat Pack for One.'

It was a fleshy, pink, eight-inch Polish sausage, tucked between two hunks of ground beef. The ensemble was crowned with a pom-pom of Italian parsley.

"It's a penis," said Alan Jager, head butcher and twenty-one year veteran of Ribeye's. He was overweight, unkempt, and covered in cow blood. "Get it?"

Joe inspected the Meat Pack for One and ignored the creep behind the counter.

"Can't get away with this at Costco," Alan winked with a lecherous, conspiratorial grin.

Joe wondered if the Meat Pack might come in handy as gag gift to Chris. Just for shits and giggles. He was checking the price when he got a booty call text from his ex-girlfriend: "Tonight?"

Joe tossed the Meat Pack in his basket, bought an extra dozen roses, and sped off to his parents' house. He left the windows open to the harsh winter air and blared a Doobie Brothers CD.

Joe nearly crashed when he pulled into the driveway. His father's swamp green sedan sat next to his mom's dinged up silver minivan. What was his dad doing home from work on a Monday? A Valentine's Day surprise?

Impossible.

Rick Rittermacher was as romantic as a worn plastic bag of dried rubber bands, and money was tight.

Joe punched the roof of his car. Since signing with the Army, he'd been avoiding his father, who had forbidden him to enlist. He wielded his mother's roses like a shield and entered the house.

Joe left the car windows open, and the Meat Pack for One lay in the backseat.

Lonely. Waiting.

It was getting cold and hard.

"Happy Valentine's Day, Mom," said Joe. He set the flowers in a vase on the kitchen island, kissed his mother on the cheek, and sat at the square four-seater table.

There was a very hard, very cold fruit cake in the fridge. Fresh, hot coffee steamed in the pot. A flaking, prefab cuckoo clock hung above a wooden plaque: God Bless This Home. The floor was faded yellow linoleum.

Joe's parents, seated opposite one another, gripped coffee mugs like stress balls.

"Ask your ma how's her special day," said Rick.

Mrs. Donatella Rittermacher, waify and jittery beneath a threadbare gray cotton house dress, peered into her empty mug as if it were a deep well into which she'd dropped a cherished keepsake.

There actually *was* something down there. A memory. A memory of her mother, Concetta Mortollini, known by the boys as Nonna. Dona and her mother hadn't seen each other since a cousin's funeral two years back, and in twenty-three years, they hadn't exchanged a word, not since Dona's marriage to Rick.

As she aged, Dona missed her self-righteous mother's hard love more and more. That's what she imagined was down in that empty mug. Love.

Love and Nonna's spicy goat ragu.

"Joe," Dona made a sad smile. "Why don't you go talk to your brother."

"Chris's home?"

"Great," scoffed Rick. "Put 'em in the same room. Easier to keep track of. Peas in a pod this family, one as fucked up as the next."

Dona returned to her mug in silence.

Joe left and barreled up the carpeted stairs two-at-a-time. He knocked the rhythm from The Real Slim Shady onto his brother's door: five knocks, rest, twice more, rest, seven more.

Silence. Joe knocked again and entered.

There sat Chris, limp and discolored, like sinfully overcooked pasta. His typically clear, blue eyes were opaque with whirlpools of fear, and he wore a wrinkled coal-black hoodie with blinding white letters in billboard size: "LIAR."

"Hi Slim Shady," said Chris. He was hunched in his

desk chair, swiveling round and round.

A new release by Blink 182 was playing at low volume. In a lava lamp on Chris's desk, melancholy rainbow globs bubbled, broke, and bounced.

Joe thrust himself onto an orange beanbag like a gymnast dismounting a pommel horse. He inspected the mint-condition movie posters with nostalgia. This had once been his room.

"You kept the Matrix," he said. "But replaced Pulp Fiction with Lord of the Rings?"

Chris frowned.

"Uma the Minx," Joe shook his head, lighting a cigarette."Overthrown by Dildo Baggins?"

"Put it out."

"Chill, they know I'm the smoker."

Chris looked worried.

"That's why Ricky Retardo is home from work? You got caught with a ciggie?"

"Pot," Chris mumbled. "In the bathroom."

Chris told Joe almost everything about that morning: the stall, the weed, Paul Czernak, the anxious flush, the suspension, and finally, the wretched silence of the car ride home with Rick.

Chris left out the part about Paul's penis in his mouth. All in good time. He wasn't ready for his brother's jokes.

"Bravo!" said Joe.

"Finally another fuck-up in the family, right?"

"Straight As and Honors classes," said Joe. "You had to crack sometime. Why'd you confess to Butterballs?"

"He'd already smelled the weed."

Joe shook his head, looking even more disappointed than Butterhalter had been.

"Deny. Deny. Deny," insisted Joe, pounding a fist into

his opposite palm like rock-paper-scissors.

"You should've seen Dad," Chris said.

"Relax," said Joe. "Suspensions are paid vacations."

Atop the chest of drawers two thin-finned beta fish encircled one another in a fishbowl. They swam through the dirty water. The lava lamp glow turned candy apple red as Joe left.

Outside Chris's room, Joe bumped shoulders with Rick in the narrow hallway, and their longstanding feud bubbled up.

"Faggoty old drunk," whispered Joe.

Rick hoisted his five-foot ten, two-hundred-twenty-pound son against the wall by the collar. The two men panted, nostrils flaring like rival apes in a turf war.

Joe grinned wickedly, one hand around his father's wrist, the other grasping a clump of his flannel shirt.

"What's the matter, *Rick?*" goaded Joe. "Worn out from hitting your *wife?*"

Rick tightened his grip to strangle.

Joe grimaced, beat his father's chest, and smacked the wall, sending a dusty family portrait tumbling.

Once his son's legs began kicking, Rick released.

Inches apart, they caught their breath.

"Kiss your mother goodbye," said Rick with a resentful smile. He turned down the hall, strolling as if he were singing in the rain.

Rick entered Chris's bedroom.

"The school won't revoke your scholarship," he said.

Chris twisted down the volume knob on his speakers, turned off the monitor, and moved to the beanbag, folding his hands in his lap. The melancholy lava globs dimmed, and even the orange beanbag seemed to rapidly lose color, like a time-lapse decomposition of a peach.

"That's good, right?" Chris said, hopeful.

"Shut up."

Rick laid a hand on the chest of drawers and gazed at the beta fishes stuck in their bowl. To them, the water wasn't dirty. It was all they knew. They'd long since forgotten the clarity of the pet store fish tank where they were born.

"Christopher, your mother is fragile. She expects this from Joe, but you've…she's not well."

Turquoise globs in the lava lamp wandered aimlessly. The fish, miraculously, slept.

"You put her over the edge."

Chris slid deeper into his beanbag.

"You're grounded."

Chris hung his head. His first grounding.

"And you will not DJ that dance."

Historically underfunded and poorly attended, the West Youghiogheny Valentine's Day social was insignificant compared to prom and homecoming. But this year was Chris's chance to prove his burgeoning DJ skills. He had spent hundreds of hours learning to spin the proverbial discs, following tutorials online and investing his allowance in equipment. He wasn't involved in any sports, and school meant nothing more than going through the motions. Music was the one pursuit that made Chris feel alive.

"Dad, please."

"Enough."

"They won't find a replacement in time."

"That's not your problem," Rick replied.

"I…"

Chris saw the anger in his father's face and backed down. Rick nodded with satisfaction.

"Apologize to your mother."

Rick left.

Chris checked his friend's away messages on AIM. None had changed. The final bell at West Yough hadn't yet rung. It was last period, and by then everyone would have heard who had been suspended for smoking in the bathroom. He hoped no one had hear anything else, especially not his girlfriend, Madison Tomino.

Joe kissed his mother with routine tenderness and left the house. He walked down the frozen asphalt driveway, stained with rock salt that crept into thousands of cracks filled with dead grass.

Joe sighed with admiration as his cherry red sedan gleamed in the sunlight. He'd treated it to a premium wash that morning. His parents' vehicles, on the other hand, were spackled with wintry crust like dry skin in need of lotion.

Joe noticed the Valentine's Day Meat Pack for One in his backseat. He cursed. He'd meant to deliver the comedy to Chris, which might've helped raise his little brother's spirits.

Joe got another text from his ex: "Bring weed."

"What time?" He hopped in and thrust the car in gear.

"Now."

Meanwhile, the meaty Polish sausage crystallized against its tight cellophane wrapping. The hunks of ground chuck petrified into cannonballs.

The Meat Pack was growing ever colder, ever harder.

Christina Czernak, Paul's older sister, was a twenty-three-year-old master's student in Education with a focus on Special Ed. She was the one who sent Joe that booty call text. She hadn't had sex since graduating university eight months before. Who better than her well-hung, high school sweetheart with a weed connection to come over for a Valentine's Day bang?

Christina didn't think twice about Joe's feelings. In fact, since their unamicable split five years before when Joe called her a money-grubbing slut, she'd assumed he didn't have any.

Christina's father, Louis Czernak, was a locally famous knee surgeon who had never approved of her suspicious, tattooed, high school hubby. Cecilia Walofski Czernak, Lou's wife and former tennis trainer, was proud to have raised two children outside the tradition of the Roman Catholic Church and was prepared to advocate for abortion, if necessary.

When the Czernaks married at eighteen years old, Ceil and Lou didn't have two nickels to make a dime. Engaged on Valentine's Day in 1979, they married without ceremony a week later. They placed a down payment on a one-bedroom apartment in a dilapidated complex. Lou's career promptly took off. They moved into a suburban McMansion, and their marriage was one of the happier ones.

Each year, the Czernak's spent their anniversary at an upscale, all-inclusive resort on a sparkling Caribbean island off the coast of Belize. They humped like rabbits, and left Christina and Paul at home.

With Paul suspended and locked in his room, Christina had the McMansion to herself.

And her hot hung booty call was on his way.

After checking his friends' away messages, Chris set

one of his own. He wrote out dark, emo lyrics from his favorite Midwestern screamo band, Hawthorne Heights, and used an edgy font to get the moody message across.

Chris booted up the Sims and spent three hours building homes and lives. He used cheat codes to get money, buy the biggest house on the block, build a pool, and drop his Sim in there. He deleted the pool ladder. Sold it for $11. He watched the Sim grow tired, tread frantically, signal for help, and die. He did that a couple more times until his mom rang the steel dinner chimes.

At the table, only three words were spoken.

"Meatloaf's good, sweetheart."

Chris loathed how his parents slathered ketchup on their dried meat-turds. He ate dutifully, as though it were an unpleasant chore. He asked permission to be excused, rinsed his plate and silverware, placed them in the dishwasher, and disappeared without a sound.

"Do you think he's all right?" asked Dona.

She lit a cigarette.

"He'll be fine," dismissed Rick.

She rubbed and patted his hand.

"Rick, you're quiet. What happened today?"

Rick was silent.

"Rick?"

Eventually: "Layoffs."

"What do you mean layoffs?" said Dona, startled.

Rick slammed an open palm against the table. A glass of water fell and broke on the floor.

Rick had been laid off over the weekend. He had spent the morning of Valentine's Day at his brother's riverside trailer drinking bourbon and watching steelhead fishing on DISH network. Tomorrow he would look for work. Always tomorrow.

Dona took a long, slow drag and watched the spilled water spread into the shape of her mother's stout Sicilian nose. Nonna. She extinguished her cigarette, lit another, and gazed into the puddle.

Hard love and goat ragu.

Goat ragu.

In the Czernak McMansion, the lovebirds reunited. Joe and Christina stood at the gray marble kitchen island surrounded by white oak cabinets. Dusk spilled purples and oranges across the sky.

"Why ground Paul and stick him in his room?" asked Joe. "Doesn't he have a computer up there?"

"For once you're on the same page as my dad."

"Not likely," he chuckled.

"He called me an hour ago and told me to hide the power cables to Paul's computer, Xbox, and PS2."

"You did it?"

She smiled, grabbed two beers, and led Joe to the basement movie theater. He carried the popcorn.

"You witch," Joe teased. "I'd never do that to Chris."

"He doesn't *need* you to do that."

"This is supposed to teach Paul a lesson?"

Christina frowned.

"Let's pick a movie," she said.

They cracked open the beers and dug into the popcorn. Joe fanned out four romcom DVDs, and Christina chose one with Tom Hanks and Meg Ryan.

"Did you really hide the cables?"

Christina jammed the skip button, trying to fast forward through the previews, but the function was disabled.

"Well?" asked Joe.

"Are you here to fuck me or judge me?"

Joe focused on the playfulness of Christina's jab and missed the irritated undertone.

The opening credits rolled, and Frank Sinatra sang.

This is going pretty well, he thought. She's joking and drinking beer, and later I'll break out the joints. There's no way this is just a booty call. Frank Sinatra doesn't sing for booty calls. We'd be upstairs screwing if this were all business. No, he decided, she's giving me another shot. Maybe I should've brought more weed or some blow. We never did blow in high school.

I wonder if she likes blow now?

A Shuttle Loop is a copper-colored steel rollercoaster in the computer game Rollercoaster Tycoon. Twenty theme park visitors strap themselves in to be shot through a loop de loop, rocketing skyward for a thrill. Gravity then pulls the coaster back down the same track, and the guests disembark where they began.

Once Chris bored of the Sims, he fired up Rollercoaster Tycoon. He built twelve Shuttle Loops side-by-side, decreased their ticket price to zero, and patiently waited for each line to fill with virtual thrill-seekers. A joyful carnival calliope played merry-go-round music, and the digitized laughter of children echoed in the background.

Once the lines reached full capacity, Chris put the coasters on standby and paused the game. He entered the settings menu of the first Shuttle Loop and tripled the velocity. He did the same with the second ride but added an extra fifteen kilometers per hour. On the third, he added thirty. And so on.

Chris unpaused and simultaneously reopened all

rides in his glorious, two-dimensional park. The Shuttle Loops fired away, velocity set far too high for the length of track. Two hundred and forty highly entertained park patrons soared through the air like water jets in a synchronized fountain.

Chris propped his chin up with a hand, watching with boredom as everyone crashed and died, flames bursting across the neatly mown park lawn.

A sudden anxious pang shot through his stomach.

Did Madi know about Paul?

He messaged her on AIM:

DJ Sw4gg1N: Hey.

xMadTomXoXo: Automated response… "Ribeye's til close. <3"

DJ Sw4gg1N: My parents took my phone.

xMadTomXoXo: Automated response… "Ribeye's til close. <3"

DJ Sw4gg1N: I'm guessing you heard about today.

xMadTomXoXo: Automated response… "Ribeye's til close. <3"

DJ Sw4gg1N: I'll be on all night. Miss you. Hope closing goes okay. Love you.

xMadTomXoXo: Automated response… "Ribeye's til close. <3"

Back in the McMansion, Joe and Christina paused their romcom and resurfaced in the kitchen. They had eaten the popcorn, drunk the beers, and smoked two joints. Time for ice cream, cookies, and two more joints.

While Christina raided the cabinets, Joe sat on a stool at the island. He pulled up the sleeves of his hoodie and like a skilled craftsman, rolled a near-perfect joint.

Christina set the snacks down and slid Joe's

sweatpants to his ankles. She took his penis into her mouth and cupped his testicles with a warm hand, quickly bringing him near climax.

But Joe heard thumping footsteps upstairs.

"Is that your brother?"

Christina stroked his rock-hard erection.

"Shh."

Joe's eyes rolled with pleasure. They zoomed across the kitchen, through the living room, past the family room, out the French doors, until…

His body jerked suddenly.

In the darkness of the patio, Joe saw two eyes peeping in on their intimate booty call.

They were not alone.

"Bitches love Paulie" was a phrase known in all social circles at West Yough High, one that had been coined long before Paul Czernak's senior year.

In sixth grade at Hampton Middle, Paul was the first to finger a girl. In seventh, the first to get a blowjob. And in eighth, although the rumor didn't spread until well into ninth, the first to have sex. No one ever discovered the girl's identity. Some say she was a field hockey player at East Wilkinstown, but most thought it was his old girlfriend from Bradford Middle who had transferred to Bickley Academy.

Whoever she was, everyone knew Paul got laid.

Paul neither liked nor disliked his catchphrase and never spoke it himself. He seemed to accept the truth in it though. Each morning in the mirror he saw a six-foot three, two-hundred-pound body with firm pectorals, broad shoulders, and teeth whiter than an iceberg.

Despite his father's insistence, Paul avoided

organized sports. He was an athletic non-athlete, more interested in sports cars, billiards, and guitar. His desk was littered with well-thumbed tab sheets for Led Zeppelin, Nirvana, and Dave Matthews Band. Brightly colored Ferraris, McLarens, and Porsches covered the wall above his dresser.

At twelve, Paul learned to use the push mower. Lou showed him how to yank the cord, prime the engine, and strafe the yard diagonally so the lawn would shimmer like a country club fairway. Soon, he was doing such a fine job that neighbors solicited his services. By the summer before high school, he was netting over $200 per week managing eight lawns. He had diversified into edging, weed-whacking, and shrub trimming, too.

Cecilia created a joint bank account where Paul saved 75% of his earnings for college. The rest he spent at the local arcade on limitless tokens, laser-tag, and go-karts. One year, he got a PS2 for Christmas and slipped his older sister a twenty-dollar bill to buy him the Mature-rated Grand Theft Auto: Vice City. He even bought a brand-new Macintosh computer and a mahogany-backed Fender acoustic.

Despite his liberal spending, Paul saved thousands of dollars during middle school and had no clue what to do with so much money. Until freshman year when he met Joe Rittermacher at a Halloween house party.

Paul made a comic splash with his kangaroo costume, and his date, a junior on the soccer team, wore a sexy nurse outfit. By the time midnight rolled around, he hadn't drunk that much. But she had. They were snuggled on a worn out couch in the unfinished basement, watching four lax bros dressed as Ghostbusters play beer pong. She rubbed his crotch and asked for another beer.

Paul went upstairs, slipped through crowded hallways, and nudged his way to the fridge. He grabbed two ice cold glass bottles and had to pee. He fought against traffic to the half bathroom near the front door and relieved himself.

By the time Paul got back downstairs, the beer pong had ended and a wooing, gasping crowd had formed around the couch. His date had hiked up her tiny nurse skirt for all to see. With one hand she rubbed her clitoris, and with the other she inserted a miniature purple lava lamp into her vagina. She moaned as dancing chartreuse blobs disappeared inside her.

A few onlookers, those sober enough for shock, covered their gaping mouths. The lacrosse captain, whose square jaw seemed destined to hang slightly open to the bitter, ignorant end, nodded at Paul as if to say, "Check this out!"

Paul escaped to the back porch and met Joe Rittermacher, who was smoking weed alone in the icy moonlight.

"These parties," said Joe, passing a fat blunt like the Cheshire Cat's hookah, "are like recruiting events for AA."

Paul had never smoked. He took a hit and was immediately stoned.

Suddenly, a hulkish blockhead in an ill-fitting Kool-Aid man costume traipsed onto the porch. In one hand, he held a beer can. In the other, a ripe watermelon.

Paul looked at Joe to make sure he wasn't tripping.

He wasn't.

Mr. Kool-Aid shotgunned the beer and smashed the can against his extra-thick forehead. He grasped the watermelon like Donkey Kong holding a barrel and headbutted the tropical fruit, spilling juicy red pulp on Paul's snow-white sneakers.

Joe laughed. "Wanna buy some weed?"

Paul bought a one-hitter and two grams that night, storing them deep in the pouch of his kangaroo costume.

His date called him every day afterwards, but Paul was getting high, listening to psychedelic rock on repeat, crooning: *Welcooome tooo the machiiiiine.*

Meeting Joe inspired Paul, who used his grass-cutting money to buy more grass. First an eighth, then a half-o. He started accessorizing: a girthy glass pipe, a slender-necked bubbler, a homemade grav-bong. Paul outsourced his lawn work to two middle schoolers and applied his pioneering spirit to marijuana sales. For three years he managed a fair and reliable operation, developing a wide network of West Youghiogheny clientele, until one day it was Paul Czernak standing on the moonlit porch with the weed, waiting for Chris Rittermacher to stumble tipsy and disillusioned out of a different party on New Year's Eve, the New Year's just six weeks before that fateful Valentine's Day social.

In the McMansion, Joe's penis was still out. The kitchen was a sauna of pungent aromas: young sweat, butter popcorn, pot, and fear. Fear of the eyes in the dark.

"Paul!" yelled Christina.

Joe peered anxiously out at the patio.

"Paul!" she screamed.

"Whaaaaaat?" answered a voice from upstairs.

"Are you home?"

"Are you *serious?*"

"What are you doing?"

"Reading fucking Goosebumps thanks to your cable stealing scumbaggery."

Paul slammed his door shut. Christina, still on her knees, looked up at Joe.

"He couldn't have been outside," she reassured him. "It was a light in the neighbor's yard or something. We're alone."

Joe nodded but could think only of the sinister pupils, focused on him like a predator tracking prey.

"Joe?"

Joe couldn't find the words to respond to Christina, so his penis did. It flopped on its side in his lover's eager, practiced hand.

Christina frowned like a child holding a broken toy.

Fifteen minutes later, Paul opened his bedroom window, the first step on the journey to Chris's house. He had dressed for a wintry trek, except snow boots. Leaning lithely out the window, he extended a wooden walking stick with a loop of duck tape on the end toward the porch light. Before he could paste it over the motion sensor, he stopped short.

It had already been taped over.

But who else would have done so?

No one, he thought. I've smoked too much.

Paul secured a rope to his pull-up bar, which he lay inverted on the windowsill. He confirmed the stability of the free weights holding the rig in place and slipped out the window.

It was a starry winter night with a bright full moon. Cold, bitter air penetrated Paul's lungs, and his tennis shoes crunched in the eight inches of snow covering the patio. He made for the shed, careful to step in his footprints from the day before and the day before that. The patio wrapped around most of the house.

Had he really made so many prints?

Paul looked in through the French doors.

Joe Rittermacher had his sister bent over a maroon ottoman with flashy, golden tassels. They both wore only hoodies, and, for all Paul could tell, seemed to be having a blast.

Paul moved on. Out of the shed he procured a ladder and headed for the woodland creek. Snow muffled the sounds of the night, and Paul kept pace using the steady, patient beating of his heart.

On their first date, back in junior year, Chris invited Madison Tomino to a Saturday matinée of the horror film *The Ring*.

Madi didn't know what to make of him. Chris never held her hand or draped his arm around her, even when she gripped the armrest like a safety handle on a rollercoaster, trembling as the black-haired ghost girl crawled out of the well like a clump of possessed hair from a shower drain.

During the car ride home, Madi hardly spoke. Chris sped along to the album *Ocean Avenue* by Yellowcard, complaining that no one paid attention to "Way Away" when it was so much better than the commercial single "Ocean Avenue."

Madi zoned out until Chris zoomed in, parking at her house and kissing her in one fluid movement. She recoiled at the sudden taste of his soft, trembling lips. He apologized, and she left without a word.

Immediately, Madi called Alyssa Danville, her second cousin and best friend.

"Give him a chance," Alyssa said. "You've been annoyingly depressed since Don."

"Whatever."

Madi hung up and dropped to her knees in the driveway. She slammed the cement with a balled-up fist and wept. She couldn't help it, especially when someone mentioned Don Brader, her ex-boyfriend and first love.

Madi had never told anyone—not her mother, not her sister, not even Alyssa—that Don raped her. And filmed it. Since their breakup six months before, she'd been as emotionally stable as a sumo wrestler on a tight rope.

Madi took Alyssa's advice and gave Chris a chance, which thickened the tight rope and shed some sumo pounds. Eventually, she even fell in love.

For a while.

Back in the McMovieTheater, the credits finally rolled. Tom Hanks and Meg Ryan were married. Three joints had been laid to rest. Two sleeves of cookies had been gutted. One lengthy silver spoon poked out of an empty ice cream pint like a sword in a hollowed-out stone.

"There's never any sex scenes," said Joe.

"It's a romcom," said Christina. "Not a porno."

"It's unrealistic and unhelpful."

"You'd rather have overtly didactic movies?"

"Didactic?"

"A story with a moral lesson," she said. "One that teaches."

"I don't need a lecture, but that might as well have been Lord of the Rings."

"Because he put a ring on it?"

"Because it's pure fantasy."

"It's as old as Shakespeare. Hatred and suspicion turn

to love and respect through a comedy of errors."

"But I want to see Meg Ryan's nipples."

"Why?" she asked.

"What if they're huge?"

"And you're into that."

"No but maybe Tom Hanks is."

"This is the missing ingredient to your ideal romcom?"

"Show sexual imperfection," he said. "Make it real."

"Am I real?"

"Yeah," he said with hesitation.

"What are *my* sexual imperfections?" she asked, letting Joe stew in the discomfort.

Shortly after, they went to bed.

Joe lay under a mound of pink, high threadcount covers, staring at the constellation of glow-in-the-dark stars on the ceiling. The memory of the eyes kept him up, invading his peace of mind like needles puncturing soft, vulnerable flesh.

Even if he wanted to, Joe couldn't have thought of anything else—not the Army, not his feelings for Christina. Only those mysterious laser-focused eyes from the patio. Who—or what—could they belong to? He imagined them dancing across the starry ceiling, like a pair of murderous asteroids headed straight for him, hellbent on destroying everything he loved.

Joe was sweating with fear when Christina slid in next to him and wrapped her slender arms around his chest. She squeezed hard enough to reset a few bones.

Christina wondered why she hadn't received a Valentine's Day present from Joe. Sure, it was only a booty call, and she had no serious intentions with him. But a little something would have been nice, and joints don't count when they come from a drug dealer.

It wasn't unfair for her to expect that, was it?

They lay side by side, a million miles apart, until Joe turned over and snored.

After her Valentine's Day night shift at Ribeye's Deli, Madi made a reluctant stop at the Rittermacher household. Rick had already gone three heavyweight rounds with his favorite bourbon when the tinny doorbell rang, interrupting an evening political broadcast on the national gay rights debate. Dona put saran wrap on the leftover meatloaf and shuffled to the front door in her plaid, red-green nightgown. She smiled expectingly at Madi, the daughter she never had.

"Madi sweetie," she said. "Come on in."

Madi handed Dona a folder of papers.

"Sorry," Madi mumbled. "I've got a lot of homework still tonight."

"Is everything alright, dear?"

Everything was terrible. Madi was delivering her suspended boyfriend's take-home work and a breakup letter. She also couldn't stop thinking about rape.

"Chris's work for the week is in there. Can you give him this, too?"

She handed Dona an unsealed envelope, the breakup letter.

"You don't want to see Chris?"

Madi shook her head.

"First the queers," hollered Mr. Rittermacher at the TV. "Then the steers. Next, they'll be fiddlin' their willies into grandma's puddin'."

Dona peered over her shoulder and mechanically shook her head.

Madi smiled: "Bye."

Moonlight shone through Chris's bedroom window. He had tired of creative murder in the Sims and Roller Coaster Tycoon, so he checked AIM again. No new messages. He searched for even darker lyrics from an even more emo band to use in a new away message, but nothing was the right blend of artsy and desperate.

He left the old one.

Chris turned off the lights and played the album *Europop* by Eiffel 65. Under the pink glow of the lava lamp, he curled into an embryonic ball on top of his gray plaid comforter, like a potato bug playing dead. He closed his tired eyes, allowing his thoughts to flow freely to the music.

Without electronic music and DJing, life was meaningless. Forget Madi. Forget Joe. Forget Paul and school and games. He visualized the other isolated souls plugged into their monitors like Neo in The Matrix. He imagined that he was Morpheus, broadcasting pirate music from his computer, the Nebuchadnezzar. For two months he'd been pouring his soul into a "V-Day Love Parade" mix for West Yough's Valentine's Day social.

But Chris lacked the courage to disobey his father.

For that, he would need some help.

In the wooded valley separating the McMansion from the Rittermacher's, Paul stepped into the icy creek while carrying the ladder, and his feet went numb. The full moon laughed as he climbed out of the valley in frozen tennis shoes, shivering with each step.

Paul leaned the ladder against a rotting shed at the Rittermacher property tree line and planned his approach. In the kitchen window, he saw a distraught Dona holding an envelope and a letter. Flashing blue light in the adjacent window indicated Rick was glued to the TV. The upstairs was completely dark, except for a faint pinkish glow in the window furthest right.

Chris's room.

Paul reached into his jacket pocket to confirm he had his pipe and the weed. He clambered across the yard and set the ladder against the windowsill, steadying its feet in the snow.

Halfway up the ladder, Paul froze. A chubby, naked baby in the next house over was pointing at him.

Goo goo, it seemed to say. You sneaky bad ga ga.

Its mom burped it over her shoulder and walked into another room.

Paul exhaled and climbed further. He tapped on the window and woke Chris, who lifted his disoriented face from the pillow.

"What the hell?"

"Rapunzel, Rapunzel," said Paul grinning, holding out his pipe.

Meanwhile in Belize, on their sparkling island anniversary, Louis and Cecilia Czernak ordered a third round of Cadillac margaritas at the cabana beach bar. For dinner they'd each had plump Caribbean lobsters and bloody six-ounce filets while watching the waves soak the ancient Mayan shores.

Cecilia lay her loving hand gently on Lou's. He kissed her. An ever-smiling waiter served their margaritas in crystal goblets and handed a cigar to Lou, who lit up and tipped big.

"I worry about Paul," said Cecilia.

Lou puffed solemnly.

"He'll grow out of it, Ceil," he squeezed her hand. "Kids go through these phases."

Cecilia wasn't so sure, but since she'd never done a drug, she didn't push the point. She only remembered a younger cousin of hers whose heroin-stuffed body was found in a fast food bathroom, wrapped around the urine-stained toilet in a fetal position. Forever seventeen. No one in the family spoke of it, and Cecilia never told her husband. To her, it was just another silent tragedy that invisibly dragged everyone to Hell.

"You never wonder," she hesitated. "What if he doesn't?"

The smell of weed wafted up the beach. A pair of young lovers rolled in the white sand. They lay with legs entwined and giggled as the tide rose.

"I grew out of it," he said. "A generation of hippies did. So will Paul."

Cecilia twisted her goblet by the neck.

It was thin like her dead cousin's.

Paul hopped through Chris's window, and they kissed. The lava lamp roared back to life, blue and bubbly like a lit-up jacuzzi. A familiar synthesized voice sang about a very, very blue man.

"Eiffel 65?" Paul said. "'Blue Da Ba Dee' is trash."

"This song may not be the best, but *Europop* the album is a treasure. Blue made them a one-hit-wonder, but the underwonders are much more important here."

"Underwonders?" asked Paul.

Chris pulled up a track list for *Europop*. He played "Too Much of Heaven."

"An underwonder is a song by a one-hit-wonder that

is at least as good or better than the hit that made them famous. Eiffel 65 has a few. 'Move Your Body.' 'My Console.'"

"So, 'Zephyr Song' by the Chili Peppers is an underwonder," suggested Paul.

Chris smiled pityingly.

"That's just a song you think is underrated," explained Chris. "RHCP are otherwise famous for like ten different radio hits."

Paul shrugged, spread his legs, and leaned back on his hands. Chris opened his music composition software and showed Paul what he'd been working on. A mash-up that he had planned to unveil at Friday's Valentine's Day social.

"It's sick," said Paul.

"Hardly a symphony," said Chris. "I mixed vocals from Carly Simon's 'Why' over Alice Deejay's 'Better Off Alone.'"

"Perfect for the dance," said Paul, placing a hand on the nape of Chris's neck.

"Except I'm grounded."

"Yeah. About that."

They heard footsteps on the staircase.

"Get in the closet," Chris hissed.

Paul snuggled between a pair of puffy winter coats and closed himself in.

Ba da ding!

Chris received a message from xMadTomXoXo just as his dad stumbled in reeking of whiskey.

Rick sat on his son's bed and handed over the schoolwork Madi had dropped off.

"Son," said Rick, nearly burping. "This is important."

Chris stared at the homework folder to avoid eye

contact. The unsealed, unaddressed breakup letter was also on top.

"I'll do it all," Chris assured.

"It's important to have something in life because… they'll…they'll take anything, take it away…*WHAP*," he slammed a palm against the headboard of Chris's bed. "Just like that. You gotta find, like me I got your mom, find…*WHAP*…take *me* away, I don't feel. I don't feel anything."

Rick's unemployed, inebriated neck went limp. Nearly asleep yet still upright, he suddenly yanked the computer monitor from Chris's desk and threw it against the closet where Paul was hiding. The lava lamp turned rubber-ducky-yellow and sputtered.

"Son, here's a lesson," he yelled. "I've taken it away now…*WHAP*…ha ha haaaaaa. Don't feel, ok? Don't you let it feel…me…you. Got it? Ha ha haaaa."

Rick burped, puked in his mouth, and left.

Chris retrieved Paul from the closet, and they kissed with desperate passion.

"You should go," said Chris.

"You're DJing that dance."

Chris smiled doubtfully and pushed Paul toward the window. Down the ladder and off into the woods he went.

Alone again, Chris read Madi's breakup letter and cried into his pillow for a long, long time. He had no computer, no internet, no DJ life and now, no girlfriend.

And when it came down to it, what exactly did he have with Paul?

On the Tuesday after Valentine's Day, the first email in vice principal Butterhalter's cluttered inbox was a one-liner from Rick Rittermacher.

"Christopher will not be available for the dance."

Butterhalter groaned and sipped watery coffee from a double-size mug. He forwarded Rick's email to his secretary, the front office high priestess, Mrs. Judith King.

New subject line: "Fix this."

For thirty-seven years Judy had steered the administrative ship of West Yough High. She'd outlasted four principals and six vice principals. In the early eighties, she replaced the glass ashtray on her desk with a ringed address organizer. In the nineties, she learned how to type an email but couldn't stop banging her knee against the clunky computer tower. Over the decades, the school had become healthier, cleaner. The technology shinier, faster. And the communication, according to King, terse, ungrateful, and cheap.

"Fix this," she grumbled, patting her cotton candy hairdo. "Like I'm some trained mutt."

The complaint passed, and King's dutiful nature kicked in. She stretched her wrinkled, arthritic fingers and dialed the library to deliver the news to Mrs. Esther Rosenbaum, a tall and thin librarian as equally tenured as the shorter, fatter King. Rosenbaum was also the staff supervisor of the student-led dance committee. These administrative pillars held one another in high regard, despite their fierce rivalry for the adoration of the student body.

"Not to worry," piped Rosenbaum smugly. "I'll have it handled in a jiffy."

King smirked. Three days to book a DJ in a holiday week. Good luck, Esther.

Rosenbaum phoned her nephew, Glen Forster, owner of Forster's Music, the only local store that rented DJ equipment.

"All the DJs are booked Aunt Essie," lamented Glen. "What can I tell ya?"

"What is the cost of equipment rental?"

"$350 overnight with a $200 security deposit."

"Call me if anyone becomes available. Put a hold on the equipment."

"Roger that."

Late Tuesday morning, Joe awoke in Christina's bed, groggy from the booze and weed and snacks. Bright light illuminated her extremely pink room. She had left a note on her pillow:

> *Gone to class. Sweet rolls in the fridge.*
> *Heat some for you and Paul.*
> *- Stina*

Joe popped a sweet roll in the microwave and poured lukewarm coffee. A magazine with a jewelry advertisement lay on the counter. The cover piece was a twelve-karat diamond set in a simple, elegant rose gold band.

Joe stared at the ring, transfixed. He heard an alien voice in his head: "Buy me Joe," said Christina in flawless Baghdadi Arabic. "I love you!" The longer he stared at the ring, the more it resembled an improvised explosive device, the kind he'd soon encounter in Iraq.

I need to marry her before I die, Joe thought.

Paul emerged in a wife beater and flannel pajamas with a Beatles print.

"Ritty the Ditty," Paul said, flashing a peace sign.

"Paulie C."

Paul sat on a stool.

"I watched you fuck my sister last night," he said.

"Run out of porn?" said Joe.

Paul laughed.

"I was just passing by on the patio."

Relief flooded through Joe. It had been Paul in the dark, not some mysterious creep.

"What were you up to out there?"

"Sneaking off to your parents' place, actually."

"Oh?"

"To smoke Chris up," said Paul. "The kid needs to relax."

"Heard you're both suspended," said Joe.

"I couldn't stop laughing in Butterhalter's fat face. Imagine sniffing around bathroom stalls. The dude's a nasty motherfucker. But while I'm laughing, Chris has this vacant look. I dunno, not stoned but empty, like he saw someone die."

"Nah," insisted Joe. "He just *really* wants to be a DJ."

"I got that covered."

"How so?"

"Rosenbaum runs the dance, and she loves me. I'm going to suggest an imaginary new DJ and let Chris go in disguise."

"Like Daft Punk with the helmets?"

"More or less. But with my full body kangaroo suit."

Joe nodded. "Pretty slick."

"All I need to do is pick up DJ equipment," said Paul.

"From Forster's? You can't go."

"Dad? Is that you? When did you get home?"

"Hah. Look, if your sister comes back to an empty house, she'll be pissed."

"And you care because?"

Joe actually blushed.

Paul laughed. "Right."

"I'll pick up the equipment after work."

Paul thought it over. He'd rather smoke and watch TV, so he made a list for Joe.

"I starred what's absolutely necessary."

Joe surveyed the list. He nodded.

"Oh, and where are my power cables?"

"Good lord. You have an in-home theater," said Joe, shaking his head. "Go watch some movies."

"Right," said Paul, flashing that trademark peace sign.

The night before the Valentine's Day social, Cecilia and Louis spent a bit too long in the tequila-friendly conga line. They got tired of dancing with lumpy gringos and snuck away to a secluded section of the beach.

Twinkling stars covered the night sky like a blanket of hope, and a ferry with pulsing lights approached a pier on a nearby island.

Cecilia laid her face across Lou's broad chest. In the fine, dry sand they wiggled their toes.

"We've come so far," she whispered.

Lou kissed her on the head.

"I love you."

"I love you, too."

A dreadlocked skinny wanderer trudged along the shore, followed by a scruffy gray terrier. He carried a backpack filled with his entire life and a guitar around his neck.

Cecilia listened to the man's earnest strumming and plaintive voice. She made out a few lyrics of a Barry Manilow song, a story about blood, gunshots, and murder. But it was sung like an upbeat disco hit.

Her heartrate accelerated as the wanderer's voice faded in the distance.

"How much do you love me?" she asked Lou.

"More than the stars in the sky."

"Enough to kill for me?"

Lou laughed and tightened his grip on her.

"Someone we love," she intoned, pointing at the brightest star, "is going to die."

The superintendent of West Youghiogheny School District, Patricia Ridl Smith, rarely visited the schools she managed. Her proclivity for paperwork and lust for administrative oversight allowed her to manage the seven elementary schools, three middle schools and both the junior and senior high schools from behind a computer screen.

"Being a bitch," she often said, "is easier over email."

Those who had the misfortune of a face-to-face encounter marveled at her unusual six-foot four rail-like frame and the long, erect stick that had burrowed up her butt to replace her spine. When she did reluctantly appear in public, Smith wore freshly pressed pantsuits that trumpeted the unyielding sharpness of her personality. She also wore sleek black frame glasses, heavy rouge, and bright red lipstick.

When the principal of West Yough High announced his intention to retire at the end of the following academic year, the position had been offered to vice principal Butterhalter. Preoccupied as she was with shifting national standards in education and plans to accommodate the population boom already underway in Youghiogheny County, superintendent Smith had fast-tracked Butterhalter's application to avoid a protracted search. All that remained was a procedural audit of a school function, which was how Patty Smith arrived at West Yough High on Friday, February 17th to observe the Valentine's Day social.

Her lipstick and rouge were redder than ever, like fresh blood dripping from a vampire's mouth. The shoulders of her pantsuit were sharper than Cupid's sharpest arrow.

Patty Smith arrived hungry.

After Rick smashed his computer, Chris couldn't plan and execute the murder of Sims or patrons at imaginary theme parks, so he planned his own murder. He knew his mother had pills and that the liquor cabinet was easily accessed. He labeled this plan 'Least Resistance'. A second option was running the vintage mint green Cadillac with the garage door closed. But Dona, who was always home, would likely discover him before he succeeded. He was so useless and clumsy with his hands that he didn't trust himself to tie a proper noose or attach it securely to his flimsy ceiling fan. He had Joe's rusty Swiss Army knife and considered cutting his wrists. But his fear of blood forced him abandon that idea altogether.

Without Madi, the dance, and the internet, Chris was like a lonely volleyball adrift on the high seas. Lost, purposeless, hopeless. He spent nearly every hour of his suspension alone in his room, brooding perplexedly about Paul, completing schoolwork like an unthinking machine, and reading.

On Friday night, not long before the dance began, Chris finished reading the seventh and final Harry Potter. He was struck by how Harry effectively killed himself so that Voldemort could be killed. He wondered what that meant and found himself daydreaming about a Voldemort from West Youghiogheny who required a human sacrifice.

Pick me, he thought. Martyr me.

An hour before the dance, Paul appeared at the bedroom window with a kangaroo costume in hand. All of a sudden, Chris felt terrifyingly alive, as if every previous moment had been a divine gift. If pressed, he might have guessed that he treasured the excitement of novelty and rule-breaking, which was true. He also liked smoking weed and giving head, the simplest and easiest explanation, perhaps.

But it was more than all that.

Chris had fallen deeply in love with Paul.

And he didn't even know it.

The only people in West Youghiogheny who knew anything about Alan Jager—the peculiar butcher at Ribeye's Deli, the man who'd packaged the penis-shaped Valentine's Day Meat Pack for One—were Mike Brunner and his daughter, Julie.

One day Mike went to pick Julie up from her Ribeye's shift and wandered into a casual conversation about steak. Alan was friendly, and Mike wandered out with a novice hunting buddy.

It took three years for Alan to learn what Mike had mastered in the wilderness. Camouflage, weaponry, killing, gutting, skinning. From squirrels and rabbits to deer and elk, Alan learned all he needed and promptly disposed of their friendship.

"I'm a vegan now," he lied.

He never contacted Mike again.

Truth was, Alan wanted to be alone. Truth was, he

wanted to hunt—strangely—and alone. And in the shadow of this loner's gaze worked poor little motherless Julie Brunner, the Goth who sliced cold cuts and fragrant Munster cheese.

"He don't add up," her father had warned.

Julie worked with one eye open.

But it wasn't wide enough.

Once upon a time, Conrad Butterhalter was a Christmas Christian. A yearly visit to the stiff-cushioned pews at Gracehill Presbyterian had satisfied his exceedingly meek ex-wife, Susan, for all fifteen years of their marriage. For the most part, he too had been satisfied. The church's fire and brimstone pastor, with his dogmatic forehead creases and remorseless floppy jowls, had never sat well with Conrad.

But one day Susan mounted the citrus display at Ribeye's on a busy weekend. She stripped naked and performed an erotic interpretive dance with a seedless cucumber and three cremini mushrooms. All to the sound of 'What's Love Got to Do with It'.

Conrad flipped. He joined the proselytizing, eschaton-obsessed Evangelical Fire of God Church faster than Susan could say 'chicken fried rice'. Tragically, those were the only words she ever did say after the incident. She entered a catatonic trance and was indefinitely committed. Butterhalter had since denounced music, drinking, and all forms of pleasure.

At the dance, King stood shoulder to shoulder with Rosenbaum in the West Yough High cafeteria, which had been cleared of lunch tables and decorated with paper hearts, Cupid posters, and silly fluffy strainers.

They monitored the students on autopilot and gossiped about their boss.

"He's made extraordinary progress," noted King.

Butterhalter, ever suspicious of the student body, prowled the edge of the dancing mass like a disciplinary jaguar searching for misbehavior.

"All things considered, I suppose I agree."

"The incident with Susan?"

"That. And Smith. This is the first time the two of them have been in the same room since that date."

"That was years ago."

"Still. It was *not* pretty."

"*He* rejected *her*, right?"

"Supposedly. Not that it's any of our business."

"No, not that it is."

Paul wore tan construction boots, tight blue jeans, a chocolate-colored felt vest, white Cupid wings, and a cowboy hat. He carried a glow-in-the-dark Pez dispenser shaped like Morpheus from the Matrix, from which he dispensed little blue pills filled with molly and speed to anyone with an open hand.

The dancefloor was steaming. Serotonin melted sexual inhibition like a blow torch melts an ice block, and the students of West Youghiogheny gyrated as though machines were coming to kill each and every one of them.

Inside the kangaroo costume, Chris was soppy with sweat like a gooey newborn baby. Although he was as sober as the chaperons, his heart rate was through the roof. He twisted knobs and egged on the crowd. He doublechecked the beats per minute and stylishly held his headphones, leaving one slightly ajar.

That night, the DJ saved his own life.

Near the cafeteria entrance, Patty Smith stood with her arms crossed. She always got confused and skittish around students grinding to sexual rhythms. If she wasn't careful, the industrial-grade barriers she'd erected around her professional posture would fall like the high stone walls at Jericho. Her secret preference for BDSM porn would express itself, and she'd lose more than just her job.

Patty pretended to be busy with the audit checklist. She touched her earlobe. She curled a lock of hair. She reached in the inner pocket of her blazer for the Blue Raspberry Jolly Rancher stash that comforted her in tense moments. None remained.

Paul passed by, dispensing his little candies.

Patty held out her hand.

"They're really sweet," Paul warned.

"That's just what I need," she smiled.

Paul grinned as she took a blue pill.

"Where's your shirt?" she inquired.

Flashing lights reflected off Paul's sweaty chest, barely covered by the vest. Patty chewed the capsule.

"This is my costume," he said.

"You need to cover up."

"I don't have anything else."

She nodded absentmindedly, distracted by the strange taste in her mouth.

Patty had bought a ticket. Time to take the ride.

Madi resented being dragged to the dance by Alyssa, who hadn't wanted to lose the deposit on her unnecessarily expensive dress rental. "Just because my boyfriend gets mono," Alyssa said, "doesn't mean a girl can't have fun. So be my date, and let's have fun."

Madi assumed Chris wouldn't be there, but she still hated the idea of seeing everyone and being seen. Her emotional sumo wrestler had regained weight and teetered on the edge of a razor-thin wire.

For the first hour or so, Madi and Alyssa kept to themselves, dancing with their eyes closed. They waved their hands from the windows to the wall and whipped their hair back and forth.

A particularly filthy song by David Banner slipped through the DJ's censor, and Alyssa cupped her hands over the sequin breasts of her dress.

King elbowed Rosenbaum and pointed at Alyssa, who had begun to rub her nipples.

"Ms. Danville!" shouted Rosenbaum.

Alyssa didn't stop.

For the rest of the week after Valentine's Day, Joe and Christina slept together. Joe figured she was head over heels, so he made reservations for Friday, the night of the dance, at an upscale Italian restaurant.

Joe planned to reveal his eternal love right after they shared tiramisu for two. Throughout dinner, he thumbed a velvet jewelry box in his pocket. He looked into Christina's steely, hazel eyes and the world made sense. Her hair, her lips, her soft breasts. When her skin touched his, he felt truly alive. Yet he also feared the whispering shadows in the dark, the foreignness that awaited him in the Iraqi desert, and the likelihood of death.

"I ship out on Sunday," he blurted out as the tiramisu hit the table.

Not exactly a proposal.

"Gonna kill you some terrorists, huh?"

Every Friday night, the Rittermachers watched a Hallmark Channel romance movie: a big town hotshot rediscovers her roots and falls in love with a local yokel ex-squeeze. There are some struggles, but everything works out fine.

Dona ran out of red box wine during an aggressive commercial for transvaginal mesh and went for a refill. She paused at the kitchen sink to admire a faded polaroid pinned next to the coffee pot. It showed her two boys, age nine and fourteen, holding boogie boards on the boardwalk at Ocean City, New Jersey. Filled with glee.

I better check on Chris, she thought.

He was gone, and Dona was terrified. She couldn't know that her youngest had begun his original seventeen-minute remix of Carly Simon and Alice Deejay and was now stumbling in a kangaroo suit behind Paul Czernak toward the second-floor bathroom where they had been suspended just four days prior.

Dona assumed her baby boy was missing, tortured, raped, and murdered.

By the end of the night, someone would be.

When the wiry cross-country captain fainted in line for the water fountain, the chaperons realized something was amiss. The students seemed to bask in the smell of their own sweat, rubbing their taut, wet bodies against one another. Living young and wild and free.

Too free, perhaps. They were critically dehydrated.

King leapt into action and found the grumpy night-shift janitor, who unlocked the cafeteria supplies. She ferried crates of bottled water to the fountain area where Rosenbaum maintained order like a lioness at a watering hole.

Meanwhile, Patty Smith was eyeing Butterhalter when the Molly Rancher she'd taken from Paul kicked in. A tingling sensation sprouted from her pelvis and climbed her stiff spine like a million tap-dancing spiders. She rubbed a hot hand across her collarbone and gazed into Butterhalter's doe-like brown eyes.

"I'm gonna make him my bitch," she thought, concretizing in an instant her decades of unrealized sexual fantasy.

She completed the checklist and finished her notes on the report that would soon birth her newest creation: Conrad Butterhalter, Principal, West Youghiogheny High. She released her hay-colored hair from its straight-jacket bun, threw off her blazer, and approached her prey.

"I can *make* you," she hissed.

Butterhalter gulped. Smith's pupils were wild, wide, and black, like the long dark night. He was sure he'd lost his job. He feared she might even be a demon of the end-times, like his new Evangelical pastor had warned of. An image of his ex-wife Susan on the citrus stand flashed before his eyes.

Holy Mary, he thought. I should have gone Catholic.

No one saw Patty slap Conrad in the dim cafeteria. Nor did they see her man-handle his chubby cheeks into a tight mush.

"No one keeps me waiting," she cooed, kissing him.

Patty dragged Conrad away from the DJ stand.

They climbed the stairs to the second floor.

Dehydrated, ecstatic, and menstrual, Alyssa sidled up to Madi and tugged desperately at her dress.

"Do you have any tampons?"

Madi shooed her away and focused on pushing her butt up against a third-chair trombonist in the jazz band with whom she'd been half-heartedly grinding.

Alyssa persisted.

"I'm high as fuck," her best friend pleaded, nearly crying. "And I just got my period."

Madi begrudgingly led Alyssa towards a backup stash of feminine products in her locker.

On the second floor.

Six weeks before the Valentine's Day social, Paul first met Chris on the porch of a New Year's open house. He noticed Chris's pretty blue eyes, baby-soft skin, and sharp Adam's apple. Immediately, Paul calculated the probable path of Least Resistance to scoring with this beautiful young man.

That night, in the freezing air, Paul grabbed a handful of Chris's butt over thick winter jeans. To both of their surprises, it worked. They were soon locked in a passionate, fearful, confused kiss.

But this was interrupted by Alyssa Danville.

Drunk and messy, Alyssa was shouting from a bedroom window: "I'm gonna jump over all those trash cans!"

And she did. She also landed face first in a pile of hard snow and broke her nose.

Later, Chris blew Paul in his car.

The next day, Madi and Chris, who'd been dating for a year by then, had sex. She sensed a distance, which reminded her of Don Brader. Chris wasn't himself. His attention was elsewhere. But why?

Madi avoided the question, and that distance grew and grew until her emotional sumo wrestler was a thousand pounds. Weeks went by, and when she finally heard that Chris—her sweet, honors student boyfriend—

had been caught smoking weed in the bathroom, the sumo wrestler lost his balance and fell.

Madi knew it was over. She had to break up with Chris or risk being in love with a liar. If he lied about this, what else might he do?

A lot more, it turns out.

Ever since the New Years party, Chris had been sneaking around slobbing on Paul's knob for the whole month of January. And lately, since getting suspended, he'd been fantasizing about a whole lot more.

Back at the dance, in the second floor boy's bathroom of West Yough High, Chris stood before the mirror watching Paul kiss his neck, feeling his warm hands slide underneath the kangaroo costume's butt flap.

Paul lowered his jeans. He did not remove his cowboy hat or velvet vest. He fully undid the rear flap and liberally applied lube.

Shouts of 'Why?' and 'Alone!' floated into the bathroom from the dancefloor.

Paul started with a finger and played with it, as David Banner might have suggested. Eventually, he inserted his stiff penis.

Chris howled as though the Tower of Babel had pierced the Vault of Heaven, and Paul slapped a hand over the mouth of the kangaroo costume.

But the moan still escaped into the hallway.

The Rittermachers burst onto the dancefloor. Rick filled with righteous fury, Dona with compassionate concern. The DJ stand was empty. Only a few couples still danced. Most students were slumped against the walls, faces gaunt and tortured.

Only one chaperon, the AP U.S. History teacher Mr. Keaton, stood watch.

"What the hell's going on?" asked Mr. Rittermacher.

"A dancing sickness," said Keaton. "Hysteria swept over them like witchcraft. I've taught the Salem trials for twenty years but..."

"Where's Chris?" asked Dona.

"Chris who?"

"Where's the DJ?" said Rick.

"See Mrs. King," said Keaton.

Ambulance lights flashed into the atrium where students huddled around the ramshackle water station.

King had assembled every pallet in the school, and still they were running out. Rosenbaum tapped the face of anyone whose eyes had shut for too long. The janitor wheeled in a water cooler from the teacher's lounge and distributed boxes of energy bars and oranges. The scene reeked of misfired pheromones, copious spray deodorant, and that special fragrance of teen despair.

"The DJ. Where is he?" yelled Rick.

King stopped whizzing from student to student.

"On stage," she answered.

"The stage is empty!"

"Esther," shouted King. "Talk to this man."

Rosenbaum set down a case of Gatorade.

"Where's my son?" asked Rick. "Where's the DJ?"

"The kangaroo ran upstairs," Rosenbaum said, dismissing the question with a wave of the hand.

Rick and Dona made for the second floor.

Madi and Alyssa's jaws hit the floor when they saw vice-principal Butterhalter with his hand down superintendent Smith's skirt. From twenty yards away, at their second-floor lockers, they watched Smith stamp hickeys across Butterhalter's neck and try to force his head down to her crotch.

"Bite the apple," Smith said, pumping his bald head like a golf ball cleaner.

Butterhalter resisted.

"Eat me!"

Smith pushed Butterhalter into the girl's bathroom.

Madi grabbed the tampons and followed Alyssa toward the bathroom. They snuck up next to the entrance and tuned their ears like transistor radios.

In thirty-three years of marriage, Belize had never failed the Czernaks, but the night after her dark prophecy, the night of the V-Day social, Cecilia Czernak devolved.

Again, the backpacked wanderer passed by on the beach singing 'Copacabana' by Barry Manilow.

This time, Ceil convulsed in Lou's arms. Her legs spasmed, flinging sand across the shore. She mumbled and spoke in tongues as Lou led her to their room. After a double vodka martini—no garnish, no vermouth—she managed to sit still and tolerate a telenovela.

Lou tried to call in favors of West Youghiogheny clinicians, searching for a therapist who could accommodate an emergency new-patient phone session on a Friday night.

Cecilia, mysteriously serene, glided into the bathroom. Lou fixed his eyes on her.

"Ceil…"

"I'm fine," she assured.

And she seemed to be. Delicately and slowly, she rinsed her face and brushed her teeth. Lou sighed and settled into an armchair. Cecilia brushed her hair. She evenly applied an oat and lavender facial cleanser and a rose blossom evening moisturizer. She clipped her nails, focusing on shapeliness. Then she kept clipping, down the edges, past the white, into the pink, removing skin, freeing blood, mangling her fingers.

She filed the disfigured nubs.

Cecilia smiled lovingly in the mirror at the exact moment her son Paul, thousands of miles away, sprinted half-naked past vice-principal Butterhalter through the second-floor hallway, down the stairs, toward the parking lot of West Yough High, and into his car, where a dark figure was hidden in the backseat.

Cecilia smashed her knuckles into the mirror and screamed: "LOUUUUU!"

When the wailing ambulances arrived at West Yough High, Alan Jager shriveled like a worm against a lamp post in the parking lot. He was dressed in black: shoes, jeans, hoodie, and beanie. He wore black leather gloves and carried a coil of steel wire. Just a few car's away, he could see Joe's cherry red sedan.

Back on Valentine's Day, when Joe purchased the Meat Pack, Alan was struck by perverse lightning. He immediately took the day off and followed Joe to the Rittermacher house. Then to the Czernak's that evening. He used a digital camera with a telephoto lens to capture images of Joe and Christina mid-coitus and spent the rest of the week obsessing over them. He pinned prints to the wall of his office and drew hundreds of imitations by hand, playing with the curves of Joe's body.

All week, foul fantasies played in Alan's mind until he finally devised a plan. He showed up at the Czernak's on

Friday night—dressed in black and ready to act. He shivered with desire and nerves as he waited for his prey to appear.

But Joe never did. He and Christina had already left for dinner.

Paul, on the other hand, had borrowed Joe's car to drive Chris to the dance. And when Alan saw Paul exit the McMansion—half-naked in his Cupid costume—well, that was that.

But ambulance and police sirens had never been part of the plan, and as Alan hid among the cars, he considered aborting his impulsive plan. The risk was too great. He stood slowly, eyes on the school. Already several cop cars had arrived. It was time to go.

He took one last look at Joe's cherry red sedan, and a particular sparkle caught his eye. Curiosity called.

Alan snuck over and put his face to the window. Inside was the Meat Pack for One. It had been left out so long that its contents were colder than dry ice and harder than Alan's heart.

Alan exhaled fear and inhaled purpose.

The car had been left unlocked.

Alan slipped into the backseat alongside the Meat Pack, which had achieved its purpose. It had called its master home.

Dona recognized her baby boy's behind through the kangaroo costume's butt flap. It was waddling in panic down the second-floor hallway of West Yough High. The irritated skin of the deflowered tuckus made Dona think of Nonna's creamy, pinkish pasta sauce.

Always Nonna. Always hard love and ragu.

Seventy-eight years-old and widowed, Nonna lived

alone in the old Sicilian neighborhood north of the railroad tracks in Millville. The last time she and Dona had spoken was on the crumbling front stoop of the two-story brick shithouse that had been their family home. Nonna had stomped her worn sandals against the faux putting green that carpeted the porch.

"Is worse than mulignan!"

"Rick's a good man," Dona had replied. She was seventeen and in love.

"Protestant no good."

"We're engaged."

"Better marry mulignan," said Nonna, folding her tomato-stained apron.

In Sicilian, *mulignan* is a slur for black people. It also means eggplant.

"Mulignan no know no better."

Joe was born three years later and Chris five after that.

The spicy hue of Chris's butt had catapulted Dona nearly thirty years into the past. These memories filled her with terrible regret and resolve.

Funny, she also felt a sudden craving for goat ragu.

The day after the dance, Saturday, Dona planned a family dinner. For the first time in her marriage, she cooked Nonna's goat ragu, a triumph over Rick's hatred of the dish.

Joe, who had no idea what had happened the night before, arrived around six in an unusual euphoric mood. Christina had denied his marriage proposal and criticized his enlistment. He couldn't wait to add his parents to the list. Yee haw.

Before dinner, Joe, Rick, and Dona watched the news.

Chris was in his room.

"Local authorities say West Youghiogheny senior Paul Czernak went missing last night after an incident at the school's annual Valentine's Day social. Administrators believe the seventeen year-old Czernak to be responsible for surreptitiously distributing what they are calling 'dancing pills'—a potent cocktail of party drug MDMA, amphetamines, and methamphetamines—to much of the student body. Teachers and other staff chaperoning the event grew concerned when students started to exhibit overt sexual behavior and signs of severe dehydration. Chief librarian Esther Rosenbaum made the decision to call paramedics: 'Drugs aren't new, but mixing two, three…everything is fun until it's not.'

At school, Czernak had an interest in music and economics, and family members say he looked forward to his freshman year at Penn State. Police urge caution but say Czernak is likely unarmed."

Paul's most recent school picture appeared on screen. He wore a white collared shirt and smiled against a gray professional backdrop.

"Christ almighty," said Joe. "That was ballsy."

Rick and Dona said nothing in response. They silently filed into the kitchen and were met by a sullen Chris.

The first to speak at dinner was Joe, who complimented his mother's ragu and announced he was shipping out.

"Tomorrow at 730 AM," said Joe with pride. "Basic training on Monday at Fort Dragg in Missouri. By June I'll be in Baghdad."

Chris felt an unprecedented pain in his empty stomach. It started as a sharp pinch, then spread like debilitating nausea. Joe was abandoning him to rot in this house, to eat dry meatloaf and surf the web, alone, until the end of days. Sorrow and rage fought for control.

Rick glanced at his wife who was focused on slicing a thick hunk of goat.

For half a minute, no one spoke.

"What the fuck!" yelled Chris.

Dona had never heard her baby boy swear. Nor had she, in less than twenty-four hours, come to terms with his homosexuality.

That's not my son, she thought. That's someone else. He's not my baby boy, and this isn't my family. That's not my husband, and this isn't my house. How could I be so silly? I don't belong here. I'm not actually *here*. I want my mom. I want my momma. I'm going home.

"Relax big guy," said Joe, chuckling.

"I can't stand this silent bullshit," said Chris.

"Christopher," said Rick. "Sit down and watch your mouth."

"You watch yours you twisted old fuck."

Chris gripped a steak knife, eyes darting around the table like a cornered animal.

Joe was speechless, confounded that his younger brother had finally found the nerve. Dona stared at her plate as if she might submerge her face beneath the sauce.

Rick raised his chin and met his youngest son's eyes.

"You people are so full of shit," Chris said. "You lie to each other every God damn day. Pretending to be in love, pretending to care. Pretending and pretending and your son now is going to die, and you say nothing? It's fine, then? News flash it's not fucking fine."

"Come on," said Joe. "I'm not going to die."

"Why else would you *want* to go to Iraq? Christ, I hate you all so much. Conceited and gluttonous and lazy and unaware. Selfish! So fucking selfish! Why do we do this?

Why do we try? I can't stand it anymore."

"Ya done?" Joe asked matter-of-factly, looking at his parents for support.

Rick was too ashamed to explain the context of Chris's outburst, and Dona was lost in a soothing daydream, answering siren calls from deep within her mind.

Chris glanced at the placard: God Bless This Home.

He spat on the tablecloth.

"Fuck this home," Chris said. "God is the boogeyman, and I'm the Lord of the fucking Abstractions. One symbol to rule them all and that's *me!*"

Joe laughed out loud. He laughed and laughed and nearly cried into his ragu. His brother had always been dramatic, but this was truly inspired. Just when Joe thought Christina's rejection would be the highlight of his weekend, he discovered a new sensation.

"Dildo *fuggin'* Baggins," Joe said, starting a slow clap. "Too much Lord of the Rings, little man."

Chris threw the knife to the ground and left the kitchen in tears.

"Should've stuck with Pulp Fiction!" Joe shouted.

Spring sprang. In shock, Cecilia Czernak denied the death of her son. She fired the gardener and bought a pair of white rubber gloves. No nasty nubs in her pretty neighborhood.

Cecilia planted golden pansies and marigolds in the front plots near the driveway. She rigged a hanging bird feeder near the hot tub. A pair of cardinals nested nearby. A blue jay discovered their nest and ate the cardinal eggs.

Cecilia slathered cage traps with peanut butter and caught chipmunks that perennially ate the perennial bulbs in the backyard. More rodents would come.

By summer, Christina had moved out. Sleeping next to Paul's empty room and witnessing the slow dissolution of her parent's happy marriage was too much to bear. Two of her girlfriends needed a third roommate for their apartment downtown. The rent was high, but the location was ideal, a few blocks from her parent's first home. Not far from the university. She often walked to class, a fifteen minute trip during which wondered what life was like in Iraq.

The night Chris popped his top, Dona Rittermacher reunited with her mother in a permanent dream. She carried out her son's primary plan of 'Least Resistance'. She laid on the unloved bed, swallowed a healthy handful of painkillers, and chased with cheap brandy.

She watched Die Hard 3 until her heart stopped.

Rick was drunk at his brother's trailer.

Joe was at the McMansion with his squeeze.

Chris was busy in the next room over, redesigning his Myspace layout with a Gothic minimalist theme.

The Czernaks finally buried Paul the weekend before Memorial Day. His body was never found because Alan Jager chopped it up and used it to stuff Ribeye's Deli sausage links. The funeral was closed casket.

Immobilized at the thought of facing the Czernaks, Chris begged his father to deliver flowers and a condolence card to the viewing. Rick agreed, but he never made it past the foyer of the funeral home.

There was a live jazz ensemble next to the posterboard of Paul's childhood photos. The musicians wore tight-fitting black cocktail attire and played Barry

Manilow. A few couples slow danced.

Rick set the flowers and card on a table in the lobby. He spit on the floor as he left.

"Who dances for death?"

Dona's funeral was comparatively morose. To the horror of many, most of whom had never met the old bat, Nonna spoke. She stood cockeyed on the grassy cemetery hillside, balanced on stubby feet covered in gruesome bunions. She was umbrellaless under a pesky drizzle and held her hands stately against her paunch.

"My girl, good girl," she began, as if from a pulpit on Mt. Sinai. "I teach her cook, I teach her make pasta, make sauce. I brush hair. Good girl. I tell her, no marry this man. This man, no. No!"

Nonna thrust a grubby finger at Rick Rittermacher.

Lightning split the sky, and thunder shook the earth.

"This no good. Better marry Ray. Ray Mulignan. I tell her then, I tell her now. Today, Ray own movie theater and two car wash. Five kid. Two house. Mulignan, but good mulignan. Not like this no good."

Nonna spat in Rick's direction.

"Twenty year we no talk, my baby. Now she in Hell. What she expect, this man."

The pallbearers lowered the casket, over which Nonna dropped a single red rose.

"Better mulignan."

On Labor Day weekend, nearly six months after the dance, Chris Rittermacher walked into Ribeye's Deli.

At the sight of her ex, Madi ran into the deli cooler and collapsed on a milk crate. She huffed desperate, tense breaths and wept. Goosebumps rippled over her. Her thoughts spiraled in a precarious double helix around Chris and Don, Chris and Don. Love was a memory heavy with fear and hate, and Madi's futureless heart froze into a lump and died.

Cautious, motherless Julie Brunner—the Goth whose father had taught Alan how to kill—was on shift in the deli, too. She sported a brand-new pair of ultra-thin, skin-colored gauges at which customers snuck furtive glances. Julie loved that her bone-white earlobes looked like fleshy gymnastic rings and savored with delicate pleasure every set of uncomfortable eyes.

The provolone ran out, so Julie went to the cooler to fetch a fresh hunk. She saw Madi crying and said nothing. Like all of West Yough, she had heard the story of Madi's boyfriend's boyfriend. Unlike most, however, Julie Brunner had no pity to spare.

This indifference broke Madi.

"What's your problem?" she yelled, running out of the cooler, exposing her bleeding mascara to the crowd.

All the customers whirled around, even Joe Rittermacher, who had been honorably discharged and stood on a gleaming prosthetic limb. Christina Czernak Rittermacher held his arm, at the end of which was a scarred hand with four fingers and on one of those, a golden wedding band.

Chris didn't turn. He remained focused on a Labor Day Meat Pack for Six: an imposing selection of twelve thick, bulging, Italian sausages.

"You. You are my problem right now," said Julie, her tone lifeless. "Is that unclear?"

Madi stomped her foot and screamed:

"Do you always have to be such a *cunt?*"

Patrons gasped.

Julie removed her plastic glove and forehand smacked Madi, who reached for Julie's hair, missed, and yanked hard on a gaping earlobe.

Joe limped over to separate the girls, and Alan, from the butcher's perch, licked his murderous lips. Christina, whose pregnancy would soon widen her slender body into lava lamp form, lost sight of the girls as they toppled beneath the cheese display. Deaf to the drama, Chris slipped the Mega Meat Pack into his basket.

Julie stood and gathered herself. She breathed deeply, reinserted her gauge, and surveyed the scandalized customers.

"It's alright folks."

She moved within an inch of Madi's tear-filled face.

"Your coin-operated boy doesn't exist," Julie whispered, handing Madi plastic gloves. "And we've got cheese to cut, so grow the fuck up."

Julie tapped a button on the counter.

"Number 44," she shouted. "Now serving customer 44."

It's Not Safe To Swim Today

In my mid-twenties, I dated this extremely intelligent, wildly sexy woman. I had only ever been drawn to smart girls. The smarter the better, I always felt. But this one also happened to be a knockout, the most attractive woman I'd ever dated. She was a government employee who'd been hired on a fast-track program for promising grad students. She had top secret clearance and occasionally name-dropped high-level cabinet officials with whom she'd spoken or been introduced to or even met with one-on-one. I only knew the name of her agency. Otherwise, her role was a black box. She may have had a lust for power, or at least some quality that all but assured me she'd one day rise to the top. This, in addition to her many other fine characteristics, was an irresistible aphrodisiac.

Those were charmed times.

I had moved to Washington D.C. as a financial analyst on a commercial real estate investment sales team. We brokered the sale of office buildings from one pension fund to another, raking in hefty fees on deals in the multiple hundred million dollar range. Although I was the grunt, accountable to my three mercurial middle-aged bosses, I made more money than any of my local friends, even more than some of my Wall Street buddies. As long as I consistently put in eleven-hour days, I had youth, money, a reasonable amount of free time, and this incredible girlfriend who happened to give great head, too.

It feels strange to call her '*girl*friend' when she was an early thirties, confident, successful career woman—an all-star in her prime, with a body to boot. Still, she retained a spark of girlish charm that came alive when flirting or dancing around her apartment. To this day, I can smell her lamb shakshuka. I remember how she'd prepare the spice mix at the counter, and I'd slide my hips against her perfectly round backside. Her deft hands never mishandled a knife, even as she'd tilt her neck back onto me and moan. Our desire regularly got the better of us. We'd pause, have a quickie, and get back to the business of the moment.

Like I said, charmed days. And lately, I've been wondering, "How'd I screw that up?"

There were plenty of things about me to dislike. I was work-obsessed, for starters. I'd go so far as to leave her bed well before sunrise, sacrificing the joys of morning delight, just to get to the office an hour before my hard-ass bosses. A lot of that was show, and no small amount of ego, if I'm honest. My dad had run himself to the ground with work, and I wanted her to think I was, like he had been, a sure cash bet. I paid for everything, too—drinks, dinners, symphony tickets. She must have laughed. She didn't need my money.

But I had other, more serious bad habits. Namely boozing and smoking. Four, maybe five nights per week, I'd hit this happy hour off K Street, not too far from the White House. It was a rag-tag group of soulful international types that got tossed, chain-smoked, sang their tragic songs, and solved the woes of the world one self-indulgent rant at a time. As a rube from suburban Appalachia, I viewed this chaotic, multi-lingual drama as real-life high art, and I got hooked on the comedy and the pathos of it all. My girlfriend, miraculously, suffered this habit without complaint, even when I would stumble to her place, drunk, reeking of cigarettes, but not so drunk I couldn't get hard.

Once, I fell asleep on top of her. In the act. Still hard and still inside.

That one, I heard plenty about. Though she eventually laughed. What a woman.

For all my faults, I was honest with her, and we trusted each other. She had no desire to hen-peck me into a corner, and for the six months we dated, I think she was happy. At least, I did my best to make her happy. I certainly was. Twenty-six years old, cash-flush, sexed up, and goofing off—what more could I want? *Her*, it turns out. I could have wanted *her* in my life for much longer than I ended up with. Looking back, she must have been observing me carefully, trying to determine if I was the type who would eventually grow up.

Apparently, I was not.

But that doesn't bother me. Well, it does, in a way. She was one of a kind, the sort of woman that if you let slip away, there's no second chance. I know that now, and it hurts. A lot. What hurts more, however, is that I don't understand *why*. I know *how*. That's easy. It's because I met the veiled woman, the woman I've never been able to talk about all these years. Not once. Not to my girlfriend or anyone else. That's precisely how we grew apart and fizzled out. My withholding. But I can't understand *why* I felt the need to keep it inside, why I've always tried to hide from the memory of that veil. Why can't I talk about her? Why have I hidden it from *everyone?*

It was a Friday evening in late May when the veiled woman appeared. I'd had two drafts at happy hour but left early to party with my roommates at our row house in Columbia Heights, which was close enough to walk on a fairweather day. My girlfriend must have been out of town. Otherwise, I'd have walked toward her place in the exact opposite direction. But that night, I strolled through the early summer heat with a carefree step. I had just passed through the gayborhood on 17th Street when I got a call from an old high school buddy, looking to catch up. I found a bench in this small triangular park nearby and listened to my friend's nostalgic ramblings. It was dusk. I lit a cigarette and watched puppies play in the dog park across the way.

Maybe five minutes later, a veiled woman sat on the bench opposite me, the only other one in this tiny park. When I say veiled, I mean veiled. Head-to-toe. All black. Only a pencil-thin slit for eyes, like the helmet of a medieval suit of armor. The kind of garb you'd expect in Saudi Arabia or some other hard-line Middle Eastern country. This wasn't exactly unheard of in D.C. But a fully-veiled woman visiting a tiny park at dusk, *alone?* One who then flips open a black hardcover tome thicker than most Bibles?

I hung up on my friend.

I ought to have snuck glances with my peripheral vision, but I couldn't help staring directly at her. There was something deeply unsettling about the total black stillness of her veil. The quality of the fabric, maybe. Or the delicate precision of the stitching. Something other-worldly in its utter perfection. Though she never looked up from the page, I knew that she sensed my gaze, and this thrilled me. I felt a hot tingling sensation around my neck and wanted so badly to know whether she felt the same. Or anything at all. But there was no doubt in my mind, or my heart, that she had at least *sensed* my presence. She knew I was there, staring.

Eventually, she left. Had she stayed fifteen or forty-five minutes? Sundown was near but incomplete. I was crushed. I'd been hoping to speak with her, or to at least learn something more from observation. It's hard to put into words, but I no longer felt like myself just then. It was as if I'd forgotten to put on part of my personality that morning, and it was sitting on top of my dresser at home, like a lonely unpaired sock separated from its natural partner.

In frustrating, absurd, or terrifying moments, I always called my girlfriend. It was one of the good habits I had developed. When these situations occurred around me, or to me, I could always count on her ear and support. And her quick wit and sharp sense of humor, too.

"That is *not* normal," she'd confirm, usually with a little laugh.

Or it's not right or reasonable or fair. Those few words were all it took to bring me back down to earth. No matter the circumstance. I trusted her more than my family or friends. And not only because she was smart. I really felt that she was on my side, even when she was critical or explaining how I might be at fault. Maybe it wasn't healthy how much I relied on her, but that's how I was back then.

But that night, once the veiled woman left, I didn't call. I let my discomfort stew, and I didn't call the next night either. I never called.

Instead, I started going to the park every day. That

first weekend, I visited four separate times on Saturday and six on Sunday. During the week, I left work early and stayed until sundown each night. After a while, though, I accepted that she only ever appeared on Fridays at dusk. If I left the office right at five (and skipped happy hour), I'd end up waiting alone on that bench, watching dog dads mingle across the way. I'd check my watch, hoping to precisely time the veiled woman's arrival, but I never succeeded. If, just before she arrived, I happened to mark the time, I'd forget the moment I saw her. Or, if she suddenly appeared out of nowhere, as she tended to do, I'd neglect to check my watch. It was impossible. Her presence was mesmerizing. It seemed to condense my senses into a hyper-focused oblivion. That's the best I can put it. The experience was unnerving yet calming, vague but concrete, swirling with paradox and contradiction, like a pair of irreconcilable Ideas.

I lied to my girlfriend about my activities. I'm not proud of that, but it's what I did. I started to think I was ashamed, deeply ashamed that I'd felt some inappropriate desire for this uniquely off-limits, devoutly religious stranger. But I never told my roommates either, which, if it were just some passing filthy sexual thought, I'd have done casually. Or at least mentioned it to my brother or any of my old buddies. If I had, the whole encounter would have fallen effortlessly into a whirlwind of low-brow male humor that characterized so many of those relationships. And *poof!* It would have been normalized, mocked, and largely glossed over, except in those rare "remember that one time..." moments.

But I chose not to share. I've never even dared to tell a stranger in an airport bar or my father when he's drunk or a competent therapist. For Christ's sake, *you're* the first person I've told, and now I'm terrified. I'm scared that she'll reappear, and I'm equally scared that I'll never see her again. All these years, it's been agony, like a rusty screw slowly, *ever so slowly*, twisting into the soft flesh of my palm.

The weekend after her initial appearance, that Saturday, my roommates and I hosted a party with too many friends of friends of friends, one of whom brought too much cocaine. Someone peed on my mattress, and my one roommate slept on the picnic bench in our backyard. The only physical damage was a broken banister. It had been ripped off the wall. No one got arrested, thankfully. The next day was a slow, painful recovery, and the day after that, on the way home from work, my other roommate got t-boned by a pick-up truck. He spent a night in the hospital. Our household, if you could call it that, had been pretty shaken up. Luckily, this pushed the veiled woman out of my mind.

On Wednesday night, my girlfriend and I met for drinks at her favorite bar, a speakeasy off DuPont Circle called Rinconcito's. It was a tiny, dim, 1920s retro joint, accessible only by an oft-malfunctioning two-person elevator. My girlfriend had befriended the owner, Bruno Odorex, who also happened to tend bar and wait tables, too. The guy was a master at working a room and a real character, always dressed in understated but highly elegant clothing that formed an eye-catching ensemble. It was as if he managed to pick outfits that projected all the fine qualities of a tuxedo without any of the pomp or pretense. As far as speakeasies go, this place was top-notch, and the prices reflected as much.

It had been over a week since we'd seen each other, my girlfriend and I. Pretty unusual for us at that point. I had expected to hear about her trip, knock a few back, head to hers, and join our bodies in that passion that seemed to define our relationship. But that wasn't how things turned out, and although it wouldn't have altered the finale, I'm certain that stopping for a draft and six smokes at happy hour *before* meeting up with her didn't help.

Why is it always *smell* that lingers?

Reeking tobacco. Spicy shakshuka. Fresh, piny rosemary.

It's why she often chose Rinconcito's, because Bruno *insisted* on serving every gin and tonic with a long sprig of fresh rosemary. Apparently, this olfactory garnish accentuated the natural flavors of the spirit. *"Ohl-fak-shon,"* he'd say, making uncomfortable, bulging eye contact with me, *"ees bery bery eem-portant!"* Then he'd smile at my girlfriend as if they'd just shared a secret and disappear behind the bar. Bruno was gay. I'm certain. That's why I never felt any type of way about his intimate tone and touchiness toward her. I did, however, wonder if he weren't dropping some strange clue.

Ohl-fak-shon, I'd think. What was I missing?

A lot, it turns out. Halfway through the second gin and tonic, my girlfriend burst into tears. Quiet tears, but they fell like two gushing waterfalls. I turned to stone. I'd never been involved in a public scene. Not that it was a terribly public place. It was a windowless space on the third floor of a disused building, and like I said, it was dimly lit. In fact, it was so shadowy I had to hold the menu up to the candles just to read the drink list. No one was going to see us in that light. Besides, we had a corner booth, tucked neatly away from the bar.

I'm sure I comforted her, put my arm around her,

reassured her, and listened to what was on her mind. Back then, I wasn't all that emotionally available, but I wasn't a bad guy either. I wasn't out to hurt anyone. Really. But as I think back, I can't for the life of me remember what had caused her so much grief. I only remember wanting her to feel better. Or did I just want her to stop crying in public? I don't know. I guess that says it all. I've always felt I missed a key learning experience that night. Some crucial piece of information got left behind.

After that, our relationship changed. Of course, I wasn't aware of it then. That night we both went home alone. We didn't text the next day or the Friday after. And just when I should have been wondering what was on my girlfriend's mind, I stumbled from happy hour to the bench, where I once again met the veiled woman.

Or, more precisely, I *encountered* her.

We didn't *meet*. Not for some weeks.

That Friday, I'd had four drafts and a few shots of whiskey, too. While the veiled woman read silently, I smoked and smoked, lighting the next fresh tip with the previous still-burning butt. Maybe I was drunk enough not to care, or I'd happened upon some courage, or just lost the good sense to heed my own shame. Whatever it was, I moved as close as possible to her while remaining on my bench. I stared and stared and craned my neck attempting to read the book. How long did I do this? The whole time she sat there. But, as I've mentioned, time didn't work right in that park. It could have been hours, but the sun never set. And I kept on staring.

I started to wonder what type of body she had. The veil and its full drapings concealed nearly everything, especially because of her broad shoulders and wide hips.

She couldn't be obese. That much I could tell. But plump or thin? Anything was possible. Her breasts were somewhere in the average size range, but, again, I couldn't exactly discern the boundaries of their form. I got frustrated. Not that I couldn't tell, but that I even *wanted* to know in the first place. Why should I have this curiosity? Who cares about this woman's body or her hair color? Why should I want to know the shape of her ears or the size of her nose? My frustration turned to self-reproach and then anger. Finally, I resented her. How dare she appear like this, under such a veil, in such an audacious display of public inaccessibility? What could she possibly hope to attain by this stunt?

I was certainly drunk, because my already muddled thoughts reared back onto me, my own presence in the park, and my attire. A lone twenty-something man in an expensive gray suit and the light brown loafers so typical among my hip, young professional peers. Starched white shirt and a pink cloth tie patterned by little green diamonds. Smoking and smoking. Didn't I have something to prove, too? Sitting there, alone on the bench next to her? Why hadn't I brought a book of my own?

I started to feel slimy, as if I hadn't bathed in days, and sweaty, oily pus was festering in every single pore of my skin. That wouldn't have been such a strange feeling in the humid months of July or August, especially in my suit. But this sensation had nothing to do with formal wear or weather. It had crawled out from deep inside me, like some subterranean insect, scattering nervously under bright light.

And just like that, she was gone. I'd been too distracted to notice when or how, or in which direction she'd escaped. But she was gone.

This time, I immediately called my girlfriend. I didn't explain why, but I asked to come over. We had intense sex that night, more so than usual. She had always been the more adventurous one, the naughtier of the two of us. But I really exhausted her, and she took notice. She must have been trying to make sense of my behavior. Maybe in relation to my stone-cold reaction to her crying at Rinconcito's.

"This is a new you," she said.

Her tone suggested I had something to explain. I shrugged my shoulders. Not to intentionally lie or withhold information or cause trouble. I just didn't want to talk about the veiled woman. I was afraid to attempt to put it into words, and I didn't know how to tell her that. Only now am I able to state with certainty that the sliminess I'd felt and my sex drive were related. How? God only knows. But back then, the sensations were all too novel and frightening. Maybe even shameful or wicked. I must have decided that that particular can of doubt needed to remain closed, that no good could come from haphazardly prying open its rusty tin lid.

I regret it. Maybe we could have talked it out. Maybe I didn't need to feel so afraid or ashamed or whatever I did feel. After all, I had trusted her wholly up to that point. But that's over now. In the end, we grew further apart, albeit in a strange way. The relationship actually *intensified* before it dissolved, like the final burst of a magnificent firework.

Two weeks later, there must have been a federal or national holiday. We had a Monday off. On a whim, I invited my girlfriend to visit my family's lake house in Chautauqua, Western New York. She was reluctant to cancel a trip to see her family in Chicago, but I pleaded. I was short on daily displays of affection, but quite long on big gestures. It worked, though, and we took Friday off to drive the seven hours north.

Of course, I didn't go to the park that evening, and I didn't see the veiled woman. I didn't even think of her, which for the past few weeks, I'd been doing just about nonstop.

The car ride was a blast. Truly. We were like high schoolers on the first day of summer, all joy and giddiness. We left after rush hour, so the highways were wide open. We flew. It felt so freeing to escape the city together. We took back roads through Pennsylvania, meandering through the endless green expanse of Allegheny National Forest. The sun was bright. The sky was clear. We kept the windows down most of the time. It was one of those unforgettable days that I wish I had a picture to remember. For lunch, we stopped at a barbecue pit that served exquisite, fatty, sauce-slathered brisket, and I prepared her for all of my parents' endearing idiosyncrasies. She laughed and shook her head.

"I'm sure they're not so bad."

"I'm taking bets."

It was in the final stretch of the journey, along the shores of Lake Chautauqua, that the veiled woman found me. I say 'found' because…well, she didn't follow me to Chautauqua and walk up and shake my hand. But maybe her spirit did do something just like that. I've never been one for superstition, yet I felt a chill that afternoon, a deep and violent chill that ran through my body like a sudden late-spring frost that decimates all budding crops.

For more than seven hours, my girlfriend and I had been listening to music. A typical road trip activity. Nothing weird about that. She'd played some of her favorite artists off her phone: Beyoncé, The Killers, Cher, Blink-182, Shakira. A bit predictable maybe, a bit too pop for me. But good, high-quality music made with real feeling. I could be a bit of a music snob, so it was important I respected her taste. We switched after a while, and I asked her to play some of my recent playlists, which tended to arrange themselves helter-skelter: Brahms, Biggie Smalls, Duke Ellington, Dream Theater, The Aquabats, Björk. A real mess. No clear through line. She was a peach about it, listening to my high-minded views on the necessity of breadth in aesthetic appreciation. Mind you, I worked in commercial real estate. I sold office buildings for a living. I had studied Economics in college and hadn't seriously touched an instrument since I quit trombone in the 8th grade. Nor had I ever delved into music theory or history. Yet this woman spoiled me rotten, this woman who had stepped foot in the oval office *as an employee* listened to my ramblings and asked questions and genuinely took an interest in my opinions.

Eventually, we ran out of new music to play. Rather than listen to the radio or sit in silence, I told her to pull out an old iPod I kept in the center console. It was black, thin, scratched all over, and filled with throwbacks. It was from this bank of old, buried songs that she stumbled upon the veiled woman. Or rather, I should say, from which the spirit of the veiled woman *chose to emerge.*

I don't like to talk like that, to use words like 'spirit' or to imply that such an entity could exist, let alone exert any influence or control over an iPod hundreds of miles away. I've never believed in spirits or ghosts or gods, and I still don't. Yet I struggle to make sense of what transpired and the feelings I've been left with all these long years.

While shuffling through 10,000 songs at random, "It's Not Safe To Swim Today" by Veil of Maya played. *Veil* of Maya. This was *extremely* heavy metal with elements of djent, metalcore, and deathcore—a whole cluster of gritty subgenres whose distinguishing characteristics had long since blurred in my memory. It was a singular song in my collection, a relic from a time of wide uninhibited exploration. It had been over ten years since I'd heard this music. It was brutal and intense, with visceral screaming throughout. My girlfriend was shocked. Genuinely frightened. Though my eyes were on the road, I heard her apprehensive tone.

"It's so *violent*," she said. "So angry."

She hadn't meant it as a criticism. It was an honest observation on her part. And no doubt, she was right. This song was, at least in part, fueled by rage. When I was a kid, that went over my head. Honestly. All I'd heard were fast-fingered guitar licks and hypnotic rhythmic syncopation. I was wooed by the prodigious creative achievement, the thousands of hours each musician had dedicated to even be capable of producing, let alone harmonizing, these sounds. I never registered this as an emotional experience. It was structural, intellectual, and technical. Devoid of subjectivity and worthy of praise for its form alone.

In that moment, as the sun set over Lake Chautauqua, I imagine my girlfriend decided something about me, and I can't blame her. When someone reveals an inner darkness over which they have yet to claim control, extreme caution might be the wisest option. It might be the only *safe* option. Whatever she truly felt about me, she hid it well. So well that I don't ever remember us talking about Veil of Maya again. She only asked one question.

"What," she said, timidly, "is he actually *saying?*"

I laughed. Vocalists who scream are funny like that. Does anyone know what these guys (and the rare female growler) are saying? If they really wanted us to know, would they be screaming? I couldn't remember the last time I'd even listened to this song, let alone checked the album liner to follow along with the lyrics. What the hell *was* he saying? We listened for maybe a minute until she could barely take any more. Then I heard it clearly and suddenly remembered. I growled along.

Who knows where my girlfriend's mind went at that moment or thereafter. Wherever it went, she was wise to hide it from me and to guard herself against what the veiled woman seemed determined to drag out of me.

My girlfriend pretended to have a nice weekend. Everything went smoothly. Too smoothly. She ended the relationship not long after. Curiously, the sex got better and better, more and more passionate and exploratory, the nearer the end we got. A loud final pop of our firework, I suppose. That sticks with me, that trend, as a fearful question mark on my life's road.

But what had been just a song for my girlfriend was to me the reappearance, the invasion into my life, of the veiled woman. Should I have connected these ideas? This one word in a band's name with some woman I'd seen in a park? Probably not. It was likely a silly coincidence that had absolutely no meaning, something my fearful mammalian mind had conjured in its eternally ignorant darkness. I'd like to believe that.

But, no matter how much will and effort I apply, I can't seem to change the way I *feel* about these events. I hate myself for it, for these feelings.

That night at the lake house, after my girlfriend fell

asleep, I snuck out of bed, crept downstairs, and sat in my car. I turned on the overhead light and searched my iPod multiple times for songs or artists or albums with the word 'veil' in them. I was desperate to prove that this was nonsense. But there were no veils. Not one other instance of 'veil' in 10,000 songs. This disturbed me. I had once been a great collector of music, like a dedicated folklorist, traveling far and wide through the internet and assembling many disparate treasures. Surely, there had to be some album, maybe not an artist, but an album title or, at the very least, a song with the word 'veil' in it. Bridal Veil. Shadowy Veil. Beyond the Veil. Something? But no, nothing.

That wicked slimy feeling overwhelmed me again. I turned off the overhead light and sat there in the dark. There was a blue flashing light in my parent's bedroom. Mom was up watching TV, probably. I wanted to drive the car into the lake and wait for the cold merciful water to take me.

Suddenly, I was struck by a feeling of indignation. This was unfair, the whole damn situation, totally unfair. I'd done nothing to earn this veiled woman's persecution, if that's what was occurring. Could my curiosity in the park have earned me such torment? I don't believe that. I don't think so. To this day, though, I have no closure. Only a gnawing doubt that eats up the bark of my memory like so many hungry termites.

I saw her for the last time the following Friday, the day before my girlfriend ended things.

In the little park, on the bench, at dusk. She wasn't there. And then she was. I was sober this time, but smoking. I'd been carrying some kind of low-grade tension in my shoulders since I'd recited the Veil of Maya lyrics. It had been building and building all week so that by Friday morning, I looked like a true hunchback at my laptop as I pored over financial models for an upcoming pitch. Maybe that's what forced me to act, the raw awareness of my physical pain.

"What are you reading?" I asked her. My voice was smoky.

She held her page with a finger and turned to me. I dared to look into her eyes. I don't know what I expected. Some petrifying Medusa gaze, perhaps. But they were two beautiful, blue eyes, limpid like the life-giving pool of a desert oasis, and, judging by the tiny wrinkles that formed at their edges, she was smiling.

"A 12th-century alchemical treatise," she said, "on the accounting of original and intergenerational sin and their respective journeys to and from the collective well of souls."

Sin? Alchemy? Collective well of *what?* My gut told me to dismiss this quack immediately. Back away slowly and return to Reality. I'd grown up in western Pennsylvania and lost my religion at thirteen. My own mother no longer went to church. And no one in the circles I ran in was woo-woo enough to treat alchemy as something that existed outside video games. Yet she didn't look homeless or crazy, through the veil, that is.

I inched closer along the bench.

"Alchemical?"

She nodded, "Alchemical *accounting*. I'm studying how to numerically safeguard my family's souls."

There was nothing mysterious in her voice, nothing seductive or playful or out of the ordinary. It did not aim to inspire desire, and, though I was now closer than ever to this alluring figure, I did not feel any. In fact, her tone was authoritative, humble, and kind. It was the sort of voice a beloved professor at nearby Georgetown University might have had. Whatever or whoever she was, I believed her.

"You're married?" I asked. "You have kids?"

At this, she looked down. I had, apparently, asked an inappropriate question.

How I yearned to lift her veil! I wanted to know her, the *reality* of her. All of her. Not the still black cloak that blocked my way, like some taunting impenetrable wall. Not the voice beneath the fabric or the eyes held captive in their armored lookout. It was painful just to be near her, to be so close and yet so far. But a part of me enjoyed this subtle torture, even felt I *deserved* it.

I reached for my cigarettes to offer her a smoke. This woman! A smoke! An extraordinarily foolish idea, young man that I was. By the time I turned back to the bench, she'd disappeared, and the sun had set. The yelps from the dog park dwindled, and the ash from my cigarette fell to the ground, like an unfulfilled dream I'd never known I had.

The sickest part of me, I'm now convinced, the most penetrating blight on my soul, if I've got one, is that I never once felt about my girlfriend the way I've felt about the veiled woman all these years. In fact, I've never felt that way about any other woman, even my wife, who emailed yesterday to inform me that the divorce papers should arrive next week. She didn't need to send that email. I'd have gotten the papers, next week or next month. Eventually, anyway. But she did send notice. She made sure she did.

My wife and I never had kids, but I don't regret the nine years we were married. There were good times. And some bad. I don't drink much anymore, though I do vape. My life's not empty. It's a *normal* life, a simple normal life like any other. I've lived in Brooklyn now for years, and the private equity company I cofounded partners with exceptional property developers. I may not perform open-heart surgery or solve world crises (like my ex-girlfriend does), but people need clean, safe, aesthetically-pleasing places to live in, and I'm fulfilled in my work.

It's just that one thing I can't forget. She won't let me be. I don't dream about her. No, no dreaming. And I've never seen her again (though I visit that park on Friday at dusk each time I spend a weekend in D.C.). But she'll pop up from time to time, the image of her, like a pesky chipmunk in my mental garden. When she does, I find myself wanting to peek beneath that veil. I imagine getting to know the *real* her, no longer oppressed by the mystery of it all. On those days, I'll think and think and think myself into a hole. I'll leave work, obsessed, walking here and there until I'm lost and frustrated, and I don't even realize that I've unbuttoned my shirt and half undone my tie, and I'm dragging my Armani suit jacket along the dirt path next to the enormous pond in Prospect Park at dusk, mumbling to myself and sniffing.

Sniff sniff sniff.

I sniff out the barefoot children who wish to enter the pond. They cannot hide their scent, and when I hunt them down, I leer with cruelty and bitterness. I sniff their fragile necks and take pleasure in their wide, terrified little eyes. Whimpering and pitiful. I savor the weak, shaking knees. The shattered innocence. I growl *it's not safe to swim today.* They are too frightened to run until I scream, wretched and feral, *it's not safe to swim today.*

www.storiesbybrandt.com